# Rescuing Jenny

By

Loraine Haynie

# Rescuing Jenny

By Loraine M. Haynie

The characters and events in this book are fictitious. Any similarity to real persons, living or dead, is coincidental and not intended by the author.

ISBN 978-1544660325

Copyright©1995 by Loraine M. Haynie

1st Printing 2017

2nd Printing 2018

All rights reserved.

No part of this book may be reproduced in any form, stored in a retrieval system, or transmitted in any form by any means—electronic, mechanical, photocopy, recording, or otherwise—without prior written permission of the publisher except as provided by United States of America copyright law, or by a reviewer who may quote brief passages in a review.

For information about special discounts for bulk purchases, contact CreatSpace.com.

Loraine Haynie-authorlife.com
Facebook.com/authorlife-lorainehaynie
Loraine_haynie@yahoo.com

# ACKNOWLEDGEMENT

This book recognizes the work of Hall-Dawson CASA (Court Appointed Special Advocate) Past Executive Director Connie Stephens and current Director, Janet Walden and all the Volunteers who have dedicated countless hours to the protection and support of children in these two counties in Georgia. Their time and efforts have improved the lives of families across the region and have ensured that children have a voice in the Juvenile Court System. Child abuse is the scourge of our society and the volunteers who contribute hours of research and counseling help judges make better decisions about the placement of children who have been neglected or abused and clarify situations where there is no abuse but appearance of abuse because of lack of resources and education of guardians.

*"Many are the plans in a person's heart,*

*but it is the Lord's purpose that prevails."*

Proverbs 19:21 (NIV)

# Chapter 1

The tires of Paul's black Pontiac squealed down the driveway. At the same time Donna slammed the kitchen door. She pressed her slender fingers over her eyes trying to calm the trembling. "He actually ordered me to stay away from the church," she thought.

Paul had never demanded anything of her before. Their whole relationship had changed since they moved to this small northeast Georgia town. No matter what he said, she was going to church. And she was going to see Jenny.

Paul thought he was protecting her. He was afraid she would be hurt again. He said she had no right to interfere in

Jenny's life. He didn't understand. Donna understood. She had been watching Jenny and her mother every Sunday. Jenny is a beautiful, deprived girl who is mistreated and unloved. Her family doesn't deserve her. Paul couldn't see that. Paul didn't see anything since their daughter died. He didn't feel the loneliness she carried with her every day of her life.

A shell of a woman, she thought as she looked into empty blue eyes in the mirror. "God took my daughter, so I'd be willing to take Jenny when he led me to her. Paul just doesn't understand these things. But he will. I'll make him ... someday."

She flicked on the radio as she went into the bedroom to dress. Normally it was easy to pick out something to wear. Her slender body could carry any style clothes and her fair complexion and blonde hair complemented any color. But today she wanted to look especially nice.

No matter what Paul said she was going to see Jenny. She was determined. Jenny needed a friend and Donna needed a little girl in her life. Why else had God led her to Jenny's church six months ago? It was God's will.

The disc jockey warned, "It's raining heavily at 10 a.m. on this cold September morning. Be careful as you make that drive to church."  The rain was beating so heavily against the windshield that Donna could barely see the curving road in front of her.  From the slight hesitations in the deluge, she was able to keep her red Toyota on the highway.  She had made this trip many Sundays, but never when the weather seemed to warn her away.

The little white clapboard church finally came into view in the familiar curve in the road.  The black and white sign hanging on the dogwood at the highway encouraged, "All weary travelers of life's highways are welcome to visit the Lord's house on His day."

As she assembled the necessary paraphernalia for the short trip from the car to the front door of the church, Donna gave thanks for the usefulness of the two sweeping weeping willows that stood at each side of the church entrance.  Before today, the trees had shaded the church from the sun and kept the congregation cool during the lengthy sermons Reverend McClure habitually delivered.  Now, they drooped as if to protect the small building from the relentless rain that fell on the church and on each person who braved the weather enough to enter the Lord's house on such a forlorn day.

Donna wondered momentarily why she had bothered to make the trip. It was only a slight feeling of apprehension, because she knew why --the same reason that brought her here every Sunday--Jenny. Only today she almost decided not to go in. "That's silly. I'm already here. I may as well go through with it," she thought. But she carried with her the feeling that this day was going to be different. That it would change her whole life.

She quickly opened the car door, before she convinced herself to go home. The dirt and gravel parking area had not been maintained properly and as she put one foot on the ground, it immediately mired up above the instep in mud. "May as well do it up right," she thought as she opened her umbrella and stepped out smoothing the skirt of her blue wool suit. She hated rain, but most of all, she hated getting out in the rain, getting her feet wet and muddy. Her hair always went limp on rainy days and she wanted to look pretty, in case Jenny should notice her.

The walk to the door proved to be even more unpleasant. Cars continually splashed mud on her as they passed on the semicircular drive in front of the church. It was times like this that she wanted Paul with her. She needed his support. She longed for his arm to guide her and his easy smile to comfort her. Why had she ever visited this church anyway? There was something about it that drew her. For months she and Paul passed the church as they drove to their cabin on Lake Lanier. It was a weekend get-away that she and Paul discovered soon after moving to Gainesville. They decided not to spend any money updating the cabin because they liked the quaint setting surrounded by trees with water on three sides of the property and a gentle slope to the water.

Lake Lanier is the largest man-made lake in the United States. It has 450 miles of shoreline and was initially created in 1951 by building a large dam in Buford, Georgia. As farmlands and home sites in Hall, Forsyth and Gwinnett counties were engulfed by the joining of the Chestatee and Chattahoochee

Rivers, many local residents became outraged at the Corps of Engineers for condemning valuable property to use as a water basin. Little did they know that in 30 years Lake Lanier would be the most visited lake in the country. Recreation now rivals power as the number one use of the lake. Property adjoining the Corps property at the lake is worth ten times the value of the farmlands. Homes were being built all along the shoreline and added to the economy of the counties where the lake resided.

      Donna was thankful for the creation of the lake because it was the second reason she loved living in Gainesville. Even though it was by some standards a small city, Gainesville had most of the cultural events of big cities. Brenau University, located in downtown Gainesville, had a beautiful auditorium where the Atlanta Symphony Orchestra performed every year as well as the Atlanta Ballet. There was a first class Art Museum where well-known as well as local artists held shows throughout the year. A new History Center provided access to local history and held shows of historical relevance. But Donna's first love in Gainesville was the glorious Green Street with antebellum homes on a tree-lined street running on the edge of the business district. She and Paul chose a home off of Green Street so that they could enjoy walks on the weekend, drinking in the beauty of these homes used now as businesses. Thankfully, they had been protected by the Historical Registry and would always remain as they looked back in the 1930's and '40's.

Atlanta is approximately an hour south of Gainesville and the Blue Ridge Mountains run along the horizon about 2 hours north of Gainesville.

Donna was not thinking of these things at the moment. Because of the rainy weather, the church was not very crowded. Donna decided to sit behind Jenny and her mother, rather than in her usual place across the aisle. Maybe she could hear part of their conversation, or maybe Jenny would turn around and look at her.

Reverend McClure had not entered the sanctuary and, therefore, there were the usual whispered conversations going on in the church. Donna leaned forward to put her purse on the cold, hardwood floor, when she saw Jenny's mother--that meek looking woman—grab Jenny's cheeks between her thumb and forefinger; lean oh so close to that angelic face and whisper something she couldn't hear.  But it must have been awful because tears streamed down Jenny's cheeks.

Stunned, Donna sat up with eyes wide and unbelieving.  After this attack, every move the child made, slightly shifting her weight from one side to the other, swinging her foot back and forth, casting a side-look at some other person in the small, barren church, or merely moving an arm, brought a similar remark and a quietly well-placed slap on the leg.  Every attack by the parent bullied the child into further action.

Donna had always found it hard to keep her mind on the reverend's sermons.  She somehow got lost in his, "And Ah, the Lord Jesus Christ, Ah, can Ah, come into your life, Ah, and help you, Ah, deliver you, Ah, from Ah all your, Ah, sins, Ah" and never could concentrate on what message he had.  But today she didn't hear the "And Ah's" of the sermon.

The rest of the hour Donna stared at the two, parent and child, fighting their own war.  Finally, the invitation to join the church was given and afterward Donna slowly walked toward her door of deliverance.  She looked around for Jenny; but as usual, the child had managed to get away.

Just as she reached the door, from out of nowhere Jenny squeezed between Donna and Mrs. Milligan. Mrs. Milligan turned around, and in her most agitated voice, "You never know what to expect from kids these days. You'd think that the Moore kid would be a little more humble. Her family doesn't even pay any tithes. I know because I'm on the finance committee."

Mrs. Milligan interpreted Donna's look of disappointment at not being able to speak to Jenny as a companionable look of disgust and was encouraged to continue.

"You know we, I mean, the church, offered to buy their place, because it's just entirely too close to the Lord's house. Those chickens out there, making all that fuss during our worship time and sometimes the smell is so horrid. But no, Mr. Moore's too proud, or too selfish, and that's my guess, he's too selfish to sell his place. Claims it's worth more than the twenty-five thousand dollars we offered him."

By this time, they had reached the front steps and as Donna quickly looked over the grounds to catch a glimpse of Jenny, Reverend McClure took her hand, smiling from ear to ear, "Well, Mrs. Whitsfield, I've been seeing you in church very regularly here lately, but you always manage to get away before I can speak with you. I'm very gratified that you've come back into the fold. You know life has no meaning unless it has direction, and I'm glad to see you've come back to the Lord for direction."

He was undoubtedly very sure that he had been the instrument used in getting her back into the fold. But she was not interested in what he had to say; she wondered how he managed to leave out his "And Ahs" in this conversation.

By the time she retrieved her hand and agreed to be back the next Sunday (as if he must make her promise), Jenny was gone.

When Donna reached this time every Sunday, she didn't see how she could wait seven more dull, dreary days to see Jenny again. On the way home, she thought about what Mrs. Milligan had said. Now, at least, she knew Jenny's last name, and even more than that, she knew where the child lived.

That information made the drive home easier and allowed her to think of Paul again. As she drove her compact Toyota up the driveway, she wondered what her husband was doing right at this moment. She had no doubts about where he was. Every Sunday he went to the golf course to get his thoughts straightened out for the week. If he ever worshipped, it must be done there, somewhere down one of those green fairways. Or was it in the shower after, when he'd be exhausted from his walk and from carrying those extra 15 pounds.

His very sleek, very up-to-date black Pontiac was not in its place in the garage yet, so Donna would have some more time to kill. No, she must never even think that word again. To kill means to take life, to stop breth, to stop the growing process—to stop everything.

She must not let herself slip back into that depression that had come and gone for so many years off and on, and on, and on, and ... sometimes she couldn't shake it for weeks.

She's dead.  No, she never really lived.  Donna was the only person who was touched by her; her kicking inside, letting Donna know she was uncomfortable.  Not yet ready for her mother to sleep.  Not liking the position Donna was sitting in.  Or pressing so heavily on Donna's bladder that she must half-run to the toilet every few minutes.  And then finally, letting Donna know she was ready to be born, urgently trying every way possible to meet her father, knowing her mother full-well by now.  But the baby could not have loosened the cord from around her neck; she didn't even warn Donna that there was anything wrong.  Donna dreamed of the beautiful creature she would hold.  And all the time the baby was slowly killing herself.  With every contraction, with every push, with every struggle to get free and meet this world, she was choking life out of her own perfect body.

Their families believed they were running away when Paul's company offered him a transfer to this small town so far away from friends blessed with many children. But they couldn't, she couldn't, face friends any longer.

Her little girl would be three now. How could Donna look at their three-year-olds and not run? They could have had other children. Could have, but they never came.

In her life, now, she had acquaintances. No friends. Who needs friends to remind you of your non-existence? How can a woman exist without children? A woman's life is only an extension of her child's.

These thoughts had carried Donna into the house and to the kitchen cabinets. She was standing staring blankly in the pantry when she felt arms wrap around her waist. She hadn't heard Paul slip in the door.

"What a beautiful sight. My wonderful wife preparing to cook me a Sunday feast." Paul laughed as he spun her around. She pretended to struggle in his arms, but at last relaxed and welcomed his kiss. "I'm sorry, Hon. I don't know what gets into me," he said. "I have no right ordering you around. You forgive me?"

Of course she forgave him. She always forgave him. And he always forgave her. Their differences never seemed important after being apart for a few hours. They loved each other too much to let anything come between them.

From the moment they met in college at Clemson University they had a connection. She was studying interior design and he was in the masters' program studying management with an emphasis on city planning. They met at a sorority party. It had to be by Devine intervention because Donna never attended sorority parties. She never joined a sorority because she didn't want to waste her time with non-academic activities. But her best friend had encouraged her this one time because Donna's favorite local band was playing. Paul was there at the invitation of his best friend who knew that he also enjoyed this band. Neither of them danced. They just hung around the periphery of the room enjoying the music. At some point, they both moved to get a better view and ended up standing next to each other.

Conversation was easy. Paul uncovered the fun side of Donna and encouraged her to get involved in some of the university's student activities. They were inseparable from that point until graduation. They both started their careers and planned a September wedding. Donna worked in the local interior design shop in Greenville, South Carolina until her pregnancy.

"Let me help you set the table," he began chatting away as he lowered plates from the cabinet. Donna only heard part of what he was saying. She was wondering what little Jenny Moore was having for lunch.

## Chapter 2

Nelda Moore put the Sunday meal on the table. "Jenny, fetch Fred and Pa."

Jenny ran toward the back door, pushing the screen so hard it banged against its frame. She looked for any excuse to get away from the smell in the kitchen for a few minutes. Although the biscuit and milk she had for breakfast had long since been burned up with the morning's activities, she wanted to avoid the Sunday smell--the sameness of fried chicken, beans, potatoes and cornbread. She declared at this moment, just as she had done every Sunday afternoon as long as she could remember, "If I ever get to be a grown-up woman, I will never cook. But if I have to cook I won't cook fried chicken. And I won't eat any of the other things Ma makes me eat every day. Nothing that comes from a garden or a chicken!"

Jenny didn't have any trouble finding Fred. He was in his usual Sunday spot in the barn. What he found so interesting in the barn she couldn't understand. He was lying in the hay, eyes wide open, but far away. He showed his 14 year-old annoyance at being bothered by his five year-old sister.

"Why do ya hav'ta keep buggin me? I'm busy."

"You know Ma don't like to be kept waitin' while you and Pa wash up fer lunch. Where's Pa?"

"Ah, he's out in the stinkin chicken house."

This hatred was the one tie between these two who had nothing in common, except their parents. Jenny always felt close to Fred when he showed dislike for the chickens. It somehow lessened her own guilt about her feelings toward her father's never-ending work to provide for them.

As Jenny and Fred left the barn, Jenny turned back toward the decaying structure, "Fred why do we have a barn? We never have any cows or horses in it. And Pa's hand plow don't need a barn. I wish we didn't have the barn at all. A barn is a place where soft, warm animals stay. It's full of happiness. Our barn is dead."

"There you go again, Jenny, talkin' crazy. We have a barn because it was used a long time ago. But we just ain't got no need for it now. It don't have ta' have animals in it. It will just be there 'til it falls down, like everything else around here."

"What do you mean, like everything else?"

"Well, look at our place-it's a dump."

"It's like the other houses on the street. Are they dumps too?"

"It is not like the other houses, either. They have flowers and plants. Ours has dirt. An' look at our clothes. They're rags."

"Well, they don't look like the clothes that other girls wear, but they do just fine."

"Face it. We're poor."

"We're not poor. We're just different."

As she looked toward the house, she could see the highway two hundred yards in front of the house. The barn on one side, the chicken house behind, and the church as close as the barn on the other side. It made her feel safe. This isn't being poor.

Jenny loved the church. Not the sermons; she couldn't understand them. She wasn't sure exactly what it was she loved--maybe all the people, maybe just the chance to get away from the dullness of the week, or maybe it was the soft music they played. She didn't like the singing as much--just the piano, when it played soft slow songs. Maybe someday she would like the singing, when she was old enough to read the words, so she could sing too.

As Fred opened the door to go in the house, Jenny turned toward the chicken house to call her Pa. She couldn't help smiling as she remembered church this morning. She liked to peek when the preacher prayed. Her Ma had warned her to keep her eyes closed tightly, or the Lord would be angry, but she peaked anyway. And she saw such funny things when she did.

One man seemed to have an itch right at that moment. A woman, who sat next to her mother was constantly yanking at her dress, or slip or something. Another man blew his nose. A very pretty woman, sitting a few rows up, thought this was the time to put on her gloves, and hunt for her pocketbook, under the pew in front of her. Most of the teenagers found this was the perfect time to pass notes, and the younger kids waved and giggled at each other.

Sometimes while the preacher was praying, she would get very brave and steal a look at her Ma. Nelda Moore was a woman who demanded respect. Jenny tried to do what her Ma wanted, but it wasn't always easy to please her; so sometimes Jenny pretended not to hear and did as she pleased.

When she did steal a look, she tried to see what God might be saying to her Ma, hoping that he would say or do something to make her love Jenny. Jenny yearned for someone to put their arms around her and hold her close. She wanted to feel the warmth of her mother's embrace. She had never experienced that feeling. She loved to get close to something soft and warm, like the stray kitten that crept into their barn one night.  The next morning Jenny was so excited over the little white ball of fur that she forgot to do her chores.  Her mother became angry, "You must forget that nasty little creature, and think of the important things like learning to cook and care for the house.  Someday you'll have a house of yer own and you'll need to know how to look after yer husband and children."

Jenny chased the kitten away, and ran to the barn to cry alone.  She loved the kitten, but if her Ma would put her arms around her and rock her in soft, warm arms she wouldn't miss the kitten at all.

Now, Mrs. Moore was yelling out the back door, if you don't get yer Pa in here, you're gonna go without yer lunch."

# Chapter 3

The next few days Donna couldn't get Jenny off her mind. "Could it be that the episode she overheard at church is a typical form of communication between Jenny and her mother?" she wondered.

Her obsession grew to the point that she lost interest in the charity work she usually did. Jenny was a far more worthy charity. Being poor wasn't as tragic as having no one to love, or to return love. Instinctively, Donna knew that Jenny was a very unhappy little girl, but she wasn't sure she could do anything to help her.

Wednesday afternoon Paul called to say he would be late coming home again. "Hon, I've got a pile of paperwork to do tonight. I'll be a little late."

"Not again! How could you leave me alone again? Who is she?" She said, "Do you want a divorce?"

"Hey, what's the matter? Okay, I'll come home right now."

Before dinner was ready, he was there. Donna couldn't tell him that she had spent her whole week thinking about Jenny.

Instead, she told him that she was bored by wifely activities, and that she had no purpose in her life.

"You can't possibly understand what it is like to exist from day to day with nothing meaningful in your life, except what you're cooking for dinner."

"But you have your charity work."

"That's nothing to occupy a whole life! Most of the time I'm about half convinced that the children that we shower presents and food on are from economically sound families, who take advantage of the charities who give to them. Their parents probably aren't even trying to get jobs. Not trying to better themselves."

"Well, darling, you've been going to church so much lately. There must be something going on in the church where they could use you. Why don't you call that preacher, what's his name, and ask him if you could help in some way."

It amazed her that a man with such talent for remembering names of clients at Sundusky Industries could not remember the name of her pastor. Even though he had never met the man, he had heard Donna speak of him often enough to remember his name.

She wished Paul would give up one golf game a month and accompany her to church. She thought it would be good for their marriage if they worshipped together, but that was not the reason for her wanting his company. She secretly wanted him to see Jenny; she could casually point her out to him. Maybe he would be drawn to her too.

Thursday morning she called the preacher, even though she didn't think he would have a job that she would want to do.

He answered the phone in a cheerful voice, "It's a miracle that you called, Mrs. Whitsfield. I've been at a loss as to how to begin the Bible study classes the church wants us to hold. The membership has decided that we need a Winter Bible school. And I need someone to take charge of organizing the classes by age, and to contact every child in the church and encourage them to attend."

"Well, that's not exactly the kind of help I was offering."

"Oh, I'm sure you will be very good at setting up the classes, Mrs. Whitsfield. And I really do need the help."

Realizing that this would give her an excuse to talk to Jenny, she accepted.

As she dressed to go over to the church to get the information she would need, she began making mental notes of the things she needed to get from the office--a list of all the children enrolled in regular Sunday school classes, their ages, addresses, phone numbers, and a list of all the families who were church members and had children that were not enrolled in Sunday School.

The prospect of finding out more about Jenny gave Donna goose bumps. "What if her mother won't let me talk to her on the phone? What if she won't let her come to the classes? I must remember to tell Reverend McClure that I want to teach the class for Jenny's age group," she thought.

Donna began daydreaming of how she would look after Jenny, if she were her little girl. Every night she would give her a bath, including a vigorous shampoo, a manicure and pedicure. She'd powder her from head to toe and dress her in the frilliest underclothes she could find.

They would go shopping and Jenny could pick out her dresses. After all, she is big enough to have her own ideas of what she would like to wear. Anything she chose would be an improvement over the Salvation Army dresses she is now wearing.

She'd curl her hair. Give her dancing lessons. And most of all, she would love her. They would have long talks about dolls, animals, anything Jenny liked. And Donna vowed she would never curse at her or slap her in the face as Mrs. Moore had done. She didn't realize she was spending so much time thinking about Jenny, until she stopped the car in front of the church and couldn't remember driving there.

She decided to use the side entrance, since the door was on the same side as Jenny's house. Maybe Jenny would be out in the yard playing and Donna could casually wave to her. She wouldn't know Donna, but she might wave back just to be friendly.

Jenny was there, not playing though. She was sitting on the steps looking down at the ground. Donna couldn't imagine a small child sitting so quietly on such a beautiful day. If she remembered correctly, when she was that age, no one could hold her down. She was forever getting into something, driving her mother crazy.

She stopped for a moment before she opened the door, hoping Jenny would look up. Just then, Mrs. Moore's yell came thundering out the door, "Jenny, git yer damn fanny off those steps, and help yer Pa with the chickens."

Closing the door behind her, Donna stood still for a few seconds, letting her eyes get accustomed to the darkness inside the church. How could it be that a woman who attended church regularly used profanity so freely, especially at a child?

At this moment, Donna decided to do her work at the church, instead of taking it home as she had previously planned.

The Reverend gingerly jumped to his feet when he saw her. How could a man keep up such spirits, when his family went without things they needed so often? But here he was busily working as if he were the pastor for one of the largest churches in the community. This church barely provided him with a living, and instead of being more severe in his sermons on tithing, he gratefully accepted whatever the members offered.

The reason Donna had been drawn to this church was because it was small and relatively far from town. She figured there would only be farm people with very little money worshipping here. But she found out in a very few visits that this little church had its fair share of wealthy members. In fact, she realized that there were as many wealthy businessmen as poor farmers. She wondered why they did not provide for their minister in a more fruitful way.

Evidently, money wasn't the only thing lacking in this membership, because Reverend McClure had hungrily accepted her offer to work in the church.

"Well Mrs. Whitsfield, your enthusiasm is most refreshing. I hardly expected to see you today. I thought Monday would be soon enough for you to get to work on the project. As of yet, I only have two other women willing to help in this special program for the children.

"I was afraid that if I didn't get started today, I might delay the start of the classes," she lied. She had been too anxious about the possibility of seeing Jenny again to wait until Monday.

"Well, I will be glad to help you gather the papers you'll need to take home with you."

"If you don't mind, I thought I might work here in the church somewhere. I won't get in your way. I can take one of the Sunday school classes and spread the papers out. There might be something I'll need and not realize it until I get home."

"It's just that the weather's so hot. I thought you would be more comfortable in your air conditioning at home."

This moment was the first time Donna had ever thought about whether the church offices were air-conditioned. She had just accepted air-conditioning; as a way of life, and anyone who worked, naturally, would have it. And most people had it in their homes. How could it be that he had to work here in this crowded office in the sweltering heat? It seemed that September had the hottest weather.

"One thing's for sure. It would be cooler at home. But I guess if you can stand it every day, I can stand it for a few hours. Anyway, if you have the time, maybe you can fill me in on what you want done. It might help me, if I understand just what these classes will try to accomplish."

"I hate to say this but that has not been worked out yet. Of course, I have in my mind what I would like for the church to do, but that is not necessarily what will actually happen. As I said, I only have two volunteers at this point, and one of them, Mrs. Simmons, volunteered to keep the nursery. Nothing more. Mrs. Kinsey said she would furnish cookies and punch as her contribution. Neither one would agree to help with the organization. Until you called this morning, I was at a complete loss."

"I don't understand. If no one is willing to help get this thing started, why are you attempting to set it up?"

"Because the parents in the congregation thought it would be a good idea. Something to get their kids off their backs at night, I suppose, or either to keep them off the streets. Anyway, the board decided we should do it, and that the month of October would be the best time to have it."

"But all the parents who are so in favor of having the classes, are contributing something, aren't they?"

"Why, yes, Mrs. Whitsfield. They are contributing their children."

Donna was so shocked, that she didn't catch Reverend McClure's joke for a few minutes. She stood looking at this kind, God-loving, God-trusting man with complete disbelief. He seemed to be facing an impossible task.

"Here, have a seat Mrs. Whitfield. Let's do talk. Maybe you will have some ideas to help me."

Right now the only idea she had was to call all of the parents of the church and give them a piece of her mind.

"Mrs. Whitsfield, are you friends with many of the ladies in the church? If so, perhaps you could encourage them to help, as you have so graciously offered to do."

At this moment, she felt so guilty about her reasons for even being here, that she was tempted to tell him the truth. Then she realized that it would only disillusion him with the entire idea of a study group. For his sake she must pretend to be sincere in her offer to help.

"No Reverend McClure, I don't know any of the ladies in the church. I've spoken to them casually, but I don't live anywhere around here, and therefore, have no chance to see anyone except on Sundays."

"Oh, my dear, that's not true. We're here on Wednesday nights, prayer meeting. And on Thursday evenings, we have a visitation hour. True, not many people turn out for these activities, but if you were here I'm sure you'd enjoy meeting the ladies who do attend. It's more informal on these nights, you know."

"Yes, she did know. Not from having attended his church on these evenings. But from the many Wednesday and

Thursday nights she spent in her own church back home. Her mother was constantly at church. When she didn't have something to do at church, the family thought she was ill.

Through all those years, Donna rarely missed a Wednesday prayer meeting, because if she didn't go to church, her mother wouldn't let her date on the weekends. She supposed that she half-listened to the sermons during those years, although at this point she couldn't actually recall anything outstanding that the pastor of her large city church had said that was so earth shattering.

She did remember all the books of the Bible and could quote scripture, though she couldn't always cite book and verse. When she was twelve years old she felt singled out in her Sunday school class, because she was the only girl who had not joined the church. She knew that she needed to desire forgiveness for her sins. But, she thought, who doesn't wish forgiveness for anything they have done wrong? So, she told her mother that she was ready to join the church. Her mother assumed that Donna's days and nights spent in the church had prepared her for what she was doing and that she fully understood the meaning of her actions.

That Sunday morning at the invitation, she rose and walked down the aisle to become a member of the church--nothing more. Her eyes searched the church for her mother, and found her trying to stifle her sobs. She was so happy that her little girl had at last been saved.

As she stood before the congregation repeating after the minister, "I Donna Logan, believe that Jesus is the Christ, the Son of the Living God." She was thinking that now she would not feel left out. At last, she would be a part of the group. Her life never changed after that. She never did anything really wrong. But she wasn't a different person either.

She just lived her life as she had before. Her mother was a busy worker in the church, and her father attended services regularly (even though he never contributed anything of himself). They never sat around the dinner table and talked about God or religion.

She was well-indoctrinated in how to act in and around church; what should be done for charities; how much a tithe really was; that it is important to visit people to encourage them to join the church to be the tithers and workers. But she never realized she should have a special feeling for the church. She learned all the lessons, but she did not know how to apply them. And most importantly, she did not learn how to love God and build a relationship with him.

After all these years, she realized that she was just going through the motions of worshipping, just the same as these people in this small country church. They were making all the right motions, but no one felt any emotion.

It was evident that someone had to give this underpaid, overworked man a helping hand. "Reverend McClure, instead of my getting down to making lists of the children today, why don't I get a list of all the women in the church, and give them a call to see if, maybe, some of them didn't realize that you need their help now?"

"Why, that would be a splendid idea, if you're sure you can spare the time."

On her drive home Donna didn't see the sweep of the water oaks hanging over the curving highway. She couldn't get her mind off the membership and the apathy they showed. She ignored the honey yellows, fiery reds and vibrant oranges of the trees all around her. She didn't realize when the highway turned into narrow streets lined with 18th-Century mansions circled by expansive porches or distinguished by massive columns.

It was not until she had turned off historic Green Street into her modern subdivision with acre lots and third-story dormers that her thoughts returned to the present.

# Chapter 4

After dinner Donna called several women in the church and asked them to meet her the next morning to discuss study classes for the church. For some reason, she had no problem getting several of them to commit to a meeting the next morning.

She went to bed with a feeling of peace that she had not felt in a long time. She knew within her heart that she was doing something worthwhile. Even if she had started this for the wrong reason, she knew it was the right thing to do.

Donna was eager to get back to the church the next morning. She wanted to get to the task at hand and to spend as much of the day as possible near Jenny's home.

When she pulled into the parking lot the morning mist hung over the grounds like a thick blanket. The sun was moving up through the trees pulling sparkling glints toward heaven. As Donna marveled at the beauty of the morning and power of God in our everyday lives, her eyes came to rest on the structure that was Jenny's home. It was a plain square building, painted green. Donna imagined that Mr. Moore had done that to make up for lawn and shrubs, which were noticeably, absent. To a slob like Jenny's father it would be easier to paint the house green than to cut the grass. There were two windows, one on each side of the front door. There were no shutters. There was a wide expanse of dirt from the church to the front of the house.

Just as she was studying the austere look of Jenny's home, the door at the side of the house opened and a boy who looked to be 12 or 13 stepped onto the steps where yesterday Jenny sat. He stood there for a few minutes and then walked towards the chicken house in back. So, Jenny does have a brother. Donna had imagined that her parents had had her by accident and made sure that they did not repeat their mistake with another child. Now seeing a tall, slender young boy altered the picture of Jenny's family life.

While she was mulling over this new concept, the boy and his father came out of the chicken house and headed toward the truck. For the first time, Donna realized that he had some books in his hand. Why, of course, he was headed to school. But more amazing than that, the boy's father had his hand affectionately on his shoulder as they talked.

Their dirt driveway was very close to the church parking lot, so when they came down the drive, Donna got a good look at the boy and his father. He was actually very handsome. A lot like Jenny. Jenny and her brother could not have gotten their good looks from their parents.

In just a few minutes the truck was back, heading up the drive. As it came alongside the car, Mr. Moore slowed and yelled over to Donna, "Ya got car trouble lady? I figured you're not here to see the preacher 'cause he never gits here before nine."

"Well, as a matter of fact, I am here to see the preacher... pastor. I have a meeting with him. I arrived early to study some notes. Thank you anyway."

He must have sensed her put-down, because he gunned the engine. The big tires stirred so much dust that Donna immediately rolled up the window to keep the black interior of the little car from getting red dust all over it.

Completing a quick inspection of the seats, she looked up just as the truck stopped at the side door of the house. Before Mr. Moore could get out of the truck, the screen door flew open and Jenny came running down the steps, rubbing her eyes and crying. Before she could get the window down to try and catch their conversation, father and daughter had disappeared into the chicken house.

The meeting was lengthy and boring. Right now she couldn't care less about study classes. She wanted to get away and think about Jenny, to figure out a way to help a little girl who evidently was very much in need of love and understanding.

Now that the ladies were together, they were enjoying their importance of being in a position to make decisions that would affect the whole church. But they were talking about everything besides the study classes. Mrs. White was saying something about piano lessons, and how good it would be for the children to come to the church to take their lessons, where everything was quiet. And about how Miss Shoemaker would probably give a reduced rate, if she only had to go to one place to give lessons to several children.

The women decided to meet at an air-conditioned restaurant in town to finish their conversation, and thus the first meeting was ended with no major decisions being made. Donna begged off with the excuse that she had a previous commitment.

## Chapter 5

"Jenny. Jenny. Jenny. Hon, when will you ever learn? You know I told ya to stay clear of yer Ma this mornin'. She's in one of those moods. Someday when you git to be a woman, you'll understand what it's all about."

"I know Pa. But why does it *have* to be this way?"

"That's just the way the Lord meant it honey. That's the only answer I have to give ya."

Jenny had hushed her crying, and she and her Pa were sitting on two rickety stools in the chicken house. Jenny was listening to him, but he had told her this same story over and over. She still didn't understand. Why was it that just because her mother was older she had to act so differently one minute from the next. One minute she was showing Jenny how to dust the furniture, and the next, when Jenny accidentally knocked a vase off of the shelf, she was tearing into her, cursing and swinging her arms as if to strike her. The stupid old vase didn't even break. What was she so mad about anyway?

At this point Jenny needed someone to put strong arms around her, cuddle her and kiss her. She knew her father wouldn't. She had seen him put his hand on her brother's shoulder many times, but this was the only sign of affection he offered to anyone. He had never hugged Jenny. Jenny wondered if he had ever hugged her Ma.

Hubert Moore knew that right now he should show some love to Jenny, but he wasn't sure how to handle affection of this kind. It took everything within him to put his hand on Fred's shoulder occasionally. He was afraid he would be rejected. And years of rejection by Nelda Moore had firmly convinced him that it was far better to be without physical love than to take the chance of rejection.

When they were first married Nelda was a sweet, loving wife. But after Fred was born her affection for Hubert slackened off considerably. When Jenny accidentally came along, Nelda's affection died.

He wanted a large family because he loved children and to ease the workload for everyone on the farm. Hubert had hoped for several sons, and had wanted them much sooner than Nelda had permitted. True, they had married young—she was sixteen and he was eighteen, but it was almost a sin to wait the fifteen years they had waited for Fred. When she became pregnant with Jenny, Nelda showed that she no longer wanted any physical relationship with her husband. He had decided his life was a great waste. And he was positive that the lack of children to help him was the cause of his chicken farm's small success.

In his day, he had all kinds of new ideas of farming, new innovations as they called it now. He had planned a bright future for his wife and kids. He had taken her away from Atlanta, and he had wanted to prove to her father that she would be just as happy living in the country. He had not succeeded with any of his promises to Nelda's father, and therefore, old man Kittenridge had long since stopped promising to come to see the farm. Mr. Kittenridge had slowed down his law practice many years ago, but never paid a visit to his daughter's home. She had, in years past, taken a vacation once or twice a year in Atlanta with her father. But since Jenny came, she never went to Atlanta.

What could a man say to his father-in-law when he had not kept his promise? Hubert sometimes wondered how he ever managed to woo Nelda into marrying him.

That summer he spent in Atlanta would always stand out in his memory, because memories were all he had now. Nelda was so beautiful. Small of build, white smooth skin, shiny black hair, and a glowing personality. When she walked into the room his heart would pound so fiercely he thought it would explode. Luckily she fell in love with him as quickly as he had with her. Her father was completely against the marriage, but bowed to his daughter's wishes as he had done all her life. The only catch was the promise he had made to Mr. Kittenridge. The promise that he *thought* he could keep and that Nelda *believed* he would keep, because of his love for her.

They moved into their two-bedroom house 50 miles from Atlanta to begin their marriage, with the idea that this was just a step away from a beautiful home like the one Nelda was accustomed to in Atlanta. The small house had been left to Hubert by his parents who were killed in an automobile accident the year Hubert graduated from high school. It was small but just fine for Nelda because she didn't know how to cook, and had never had to clean house or wash clothes. Her mother had died when she was very young and the live-in maids her father kept did all the work. None of them took the time to show Nelda how to do any of the domestic duties of a wife.

Nelda had been sure that by the time they were ready to start having children, they would be in a larger house with sufficient help. And she enjoyed the freedom that her small cottage gave her. Besides she was so much in love with Hubert she thought she could endure anything for a year or two.

But the year or two stretched into ten, then twelve. Finally, Hubert insisted on having a child and added three more rooms to the house to make room for a nursery, living room and dining room. Nelda had given up her dream of a beautiful home many years before, and all that concerned her after Fred was born was to keep food on the table and dust off the furniture. She rarely ever did anything to make herself look more attractive. The clothes she must wear seemed to be a hopeless ugliness that could not be covered up with pretty hair. Her nails could not be polished because they stayed broken and dirty. All the hard work she had done over the years had drained the beauty out of her.

Even her language had disintegrated. At one time in her life she was such a proper lady, always knowing the right thing to say, and never using an unfeminine curse. Now, talking was an effort. There was nothing to say, nothing of any importance, anyway. When Jenny was accidentally conceived, Nelda was at first dragged into frustration and depression. As the baby began to move in her, she was warmed with the knowledge of life.

When she was born a little girl, Nelda dreamed all the dreams for her that she had at one time wanted for herself.

But she could not see a very happy future for her daughter unless she could get married to a wealthy man. That's why she **must** learn to cook and clean. She must not be emotional as her mother had been. She must attract and marry a man who would do her some good. Not a man who stimulated her physically and emotionally. Not a man who would make her give up her life to him and get nothing in return but years of hard work.

Jenny must be above emotion. If Nelda Moore only accomplished this one thing in her life, she would succeed. That's why she must keep Jenny interested in church. She would make her attend every function that the church offered. There were wealthy people moving into the county now, and many of them attended Countryside Baptist Church. If Jenny played her cards right, she could marry a son of one of the wealthy men in the church.

Nelda loved Jenny more than she remembered loving Hubert. But she was determined not to show it. Jenny would not be tied to her family by love. She must be free to find happiness with the proper man

It hurt Nelda deeply when she screamed and cursed at Jenny, but sometimes she simply could not control herself. She wondered if she were slowly going insane. Some days she would wake up in a fairly good mood, feeling good, and all Jenny had to do was walk in the room and attempt to put her hand on her mother's and she would explode. She wanted to show love for Jenny, but she could not give in to any impulse she might have. It would hurt Jenny in the long run.

## Chapter 6

Sunday morning fall was definitely in the air. As Donna looked out the kitchen window hundreds of red, yellow, orange, purple, and green leaves floated through the air, the wind being in no hurry to deposit them on the ground. Colored snow, she thought to herself. She much preferred this kind of snow. It didn't hamper movement of cars. It didn't trap you in the house for days. And it didn't have to be cold for this kind of snow.

"Just another of Nature's beauties. No, not Nature's beauty. This kind of beauty came from God. Why didn't people acknowledge it? Why did mankind give the credit to Nature? We seem to be ashamed to mention God's name, unless we are in church. Even church people give this unforgivable salute." She wondered what God thought of our betrayal. "Did he assume we meant God when we said Nature?

No, he did not. Some people did mean God when they said "Nature". Some people did not know God; did not believe in him; in his existence; in his love; in his omnipotence."

Paul walked into the kitchen freshly shaven and smelling like some very expensive cologne. Donna wondered if the well-built girls advertising the after-shave lotion influenced him to choose whatever it was that he was wearing.

"Mmm, you smell good this morning. What do you have on?"

"I don't know. Some of the stuff I got last Christmas."

Did most men's Christmas supply last them all year? If not, Paul seemed to be able to stretch his, because with Christmas only three months away, he would surely get another supply. All the nieces and nephews knew of nothing else to give him. So every year he would unwrap five or six boxes of after-shave and act as pleased over the last one as he had over the first.

"Paul, would you consider coming to church with me this morning?" As she asked the question, she was readying herself for his refusal.

"You know, I wondered how long you would wait to ask me. I'd love to, but on the condition that you don't pester me about going every Sunday. You know how I feel. I'll go just to spend this beautiful Sunday will my beautiful wife. For no other reason."

She conceded. She wasn't going to push her luck. It was enough right now to get him in the church.

She was the proudest woman walking into church. She had won a small victory. The next time wouldn't be as hard for him to agree to come.

This morning she honestly tried to listen to the sermon, for Paul's sake as well as her own. She knew Paul would want to discuss the sermon when they got home. Before she got pregnant they went to church every Sunday, and on the way home they would discuss the sermon. Paul urged her to try and convince him of her beliefs. While she was pregnant, he seemed to begin to understand. Then when the baby died he stopped trying to understand.

Donna led Paul to her usual spot. Jenny was there in her usual seat. Oh, thank God, she's here. Today, she seemed more frail, more subdued, and more vulnerable. Paul must see her.

Paul nudged Donna, "Well, the rich with the poor. That's unusual. For instance, look at that couple over there. They are both expensively dressed, as well as their children, and look behind them. That woman and her little girl look as if they don't knew where their next meal will come from."

Her heart stopped. Paul was talking about Jenny. "Yes, isn't that little girl adorable?"

"Well, hardly. How can you tell anything about her personality? And you definitely can't mean her looks. She looks underfed, in fact, downright puny."

Evidently he didn't see the glow in her eyes. He couldn't see her innocence. He wouldn't see the need for love.

Jenny began swinging her legs at that moment. Her mother slapped her right knee and whispered something in her ear. But it was ringing in Donna's ears. She knew what she was whispering in that delicate little ear. Things a child her age should not have to hear.

As they left the church, Paul ushered Donna to the car with such speed that she couldn't get a look at Jenny.

## Chapter 7

Monday morning Donna arrived at the church before Reverend McClure again. She was disappointed because Jenny did not come out of the house. In fact, there seemed to be no activity around her house at all.

Reverend McClure arrived just a few minutes after Donna, anticipating her early arrival. As he drew keys from somewhere deep in his pants pocket, she made a quick survey of the church grounds. She had never noticed how barren it was, except for the willows -- no shrubs, not even any grass. There was barely enough room for the cars to park.

Maybe Mrs. Milligan had been right. Maybe it would have been better if the church had purchased Mr. Moore's farm. Then they would have had room for parking and grass.

It was evident from the looks of his house and family that Mr. Moore's farm wasn't providing him with even the essentials. Maybe if he moved off the farm and got a job in one of the big lumber companies being established all over the county, then he could provide for Jenny. But Donna could not see that happening. It was obvious that he really did not have any ambition, or he would have seen this himself long before. And since he and his wife didn't love Jenny, why would they try to provide her with what she needed.

As they sat down to begin their planning session, Donna was reminded what a good man the pastor was. She wondered if he had not seen the need at the Moore house, so she asked innocently, "Reverend McClure have you noticed the Moore family next door? I have seen the little girl and her mother in church every Sunday, but never her husband or son."

"Yes, they are a disappointment to me. I felt that because they are so close to the church, they would be some of our devoted members. But Mr. Moore refuses to enter the church. When I've visited them he listens to me quietly, but insists that he will never come to church again. Their children are beautiful, but they are so poor. And they, rather he, will not let anyone help them in any way. So proud."

"Well, if ever I've seen a family that needs charity it's them."

"I know, but speaking of church attendance, I was delighted to see your husband in church yesterday. The first time he's been, isn't it?"

"Yes. He usually has so much to do on Sunday, he hasn't the time to come to church."

"You can't really mean that. You can't believe that. As often as you've been to church these months, you can't feel that it's okay for your husband to be delinquent in his religion."

"No. To tell the truth I'd love for him to come with me every Sunday, but he doesn't think he needs the church or God. He thinks God failed us when our baby was born dead several years ago."

"Oh, I'm so sorry. I had no idea you had this misfortune fall upon you. But the good Lord has his reasons for everything that happens to us. Maybe it was to bring you close to Him. Evidently that is what has happened, in your case anyway."

The morning's conversation hung with Donna all afternoon as she made calls to each church family with children, inviting them to bring their children to the classes. She found no phone number for Jenny Moore, so she decided she must go over to invite her personally.

She did not have the strength to face Jenny today, so she put off her visit until Tuesday when she could prepare what she would say.

Paul came home and found Donna just beginning the evening meal. He was perturbed by the delay of dinner, and went into the bathroom to shower while it cooked. Her heart was just not in this meal. She had more important things on her mind. When he came back into the room, she was cross with him and he immediately snapped back at her. They rarely had fights and tonight she couldn't cope with one. She started crying and he had his arms around her and they were kissing and apologizing, and it was all over as quickly as it had started.

"Just one of those days, huh?"

"Not really, Paul. I have something on my mind."

"Well, out with it. Whatever it is, it can't be that bad." He was drying her tears. Paul always had a weakness for tears. He'd do almost anything to get Donna to stop crying. But she never abused this hold over him. She didn't cry just to get her way.

"You remember the little girl and her mother that we saw at church yesterday?"

"How could I forget them, I haven't seen anyone that poor in a long time. Not since my field trips in college, when we toured the slums in Atlanta. Funny, how many years ago that has been, how many urban renewal programs have been started, how many model city programs they have financed and there are still slums in Atlanta. I guess there are as many as before all the programs began. The people have just been moved around."

Paul could get so stirred up over someone else's problems. If she let him, he would go on for hours talking about all the poor kids running around half naked, without food, some without parents. She had to steer him back to her poor little girl.

"Jenny's just as poor as any of those children you saw."

"Jenny, huh. Here we go again. I should have realized that's why you wanted me to go with you yesterday. Donna, this has gone too far!"

"Paul, I have to go to their house tomorrow morning to invite her to the Bible study classes at the church. I've been calling everyone else by phone, but they don't have a phone."

"Why is that a problem? They won't hurt you. You'll just invite her and leave."

Donna's mind raced. How could she tell him how involved she had become with Jenny? That she is more than just a poor little girl. That Donna thought of her every minute she was awake. That Donna dreamed of her when she closed her eyes. That indeed, she loved Jenny as her own child. "I don't think I could bear to go into her home and see how she lives and not be able to do anything about it. As long as I remain a stranger to her, I can keep my feelings hidden, but as soon as I speak to her and she smiles at me and perhaps takes my hand, as soon as I have physical contact with her, I don't think I can end it there. Someway I have to share in her life."

Paul only hugged Donna a little closer. He did not understand this fixation Donna had on this stranger, but he did understand Donna's need to be needed. He would be patient with her and, in time, she would realize how foolish she was acting.

# Chapter 8

Donna knocked on the unpainted screen door and heard a child's feet running to answer the door.

"Ma, we got company. Hurry Ma. Come on. We got company. And you know what? It's that pretty lady from the church."

Donna was so shocked that Jenny recognized her, she stood numb for a minute. Jenny was standing with the screen door wide open and very impatient for Donna to come in.

"Please, hurry. It's my job to keep all the flies killed. And if we let too many in, I'll never get finished swattin."

Mrs. Moore entered the room drying her hands on her apron.

"Well, what a surprise. What a nice surprise. You from the church? Yes, I know you are. Jenny says you are. And Jenny remembers faces."

Donna hesitated about extending her hand to this woman for a moment, and realized Mrs. Moore had left the room.

Jenny smiled, "I bet she left something on the stove. She'll be right back. Sit down."

"All right. I will. I came over to invite you to the evening Bible school classes at the church. They will begin on November 5th. That's just a little more than two weeks. Do you think you can come?" Donna had missed the schedule the church had wanted for the Bible school classes, but it was a miracle that she was able to pull it together at all.

The smile had vanished from Jenny's face. "Oh, I don't think so. Please don't tell Ma. She'll make me go, and I don't really understand what goes on over there at that church. I like the church, especially the piano playing. But I don't understand the preacher."'

"Of course you'll go Jenny." Mrs. Moore had entered the room again with a saucer full of cookies.

Donna saw there was going to be conflict so she immediately said, "I'll be teaching your class, Jenny. You won't be up in the big church. You'll be in small classes with other boys and girls your age. We'll have lots of fun. I'll read you the lessons, and then we'll sing songs, and talk."

This seemed to put a new light on the situation. Jenny's face lit up and she ran over to Donna and was almost up in her lap before she realized what she was doing. She stopped and took a few steps backward. "That's different. If I'll get to see you, I'll be sure to come. You know, you sure are pretty. Am I that pretty?"

"Of course you are. Do you know that you are the prettiest little girl I've ever seen?"

Donna couldn't help herself. She reached out for Jenny, put her arm around Jenny's waist and kissed her on the forehead. Jenny stood very still, not knowing how to react. The rest of the visit was short and uneventful. After the kiss,

Mrs. Moore told Jenny to come sit beside her on the sofa, and Jenny sat there studying Donna.

Driving home, Donna realized that Mrs. Moore had not cursed at Jenny a single time. Maybe the woman did have a little pride.

Those two weeks were the busiest Donna had spent in a long while. She saw Jenny in church those Sundays before the classes started. Now Jenny waved when she saw Donna. The Sunday before the classes, Jenny ran up to Donna after church and grabbed her hand. Donna's heart began pounding like a high school girl's on her first date.

"I just wanted you to know, I can't wait until tomorrow night."

"Neither can I, honey. Neither can I." She was gone so quickly, Donna hardly realized she had released her hand.

# Chapter 9

Somewhere deep in her subconscious, Donna knew an idea was forming. She felt uneasiness as she drove home, restless.

Paul planned to eat at the club today with some of his golf cronies. Thank goodness for time to be alone--to think. Everything was a fog. For the first time in their marriage, Donna didn't want Paul anywhere near. She didn't want to share this experience with him--or anyone.

She wondered if her marriage was in danger because of this little girl. Paul would never see Jenny as part of their lives, but Donna needed Jenny in her life.

As she slipped into a floor-length fuzzy robe, Donna tried to forget Jenny, and planned the rest of the day so there was no time for Jenny.

But before the last bite of her sandwich and the last swallow of her soup were gone, Donna was already making plans for her Bible class--another chance to ensure that she would see Jenny. Paul and I could take the class to our cabin on the lake for an outing. Paul wouldn't be interested in one child more than the other, so he could take charge, and Jenny and I would have a chance to sit and talk, she thought. The thought never entered her mind that Jenny might not be able to go. By the time Paul was home from his afternoon, Donna had already set the time, listed what they would take to eat, and copied the names and phone numbers of all the girls and boys in her class.

She couldn't take a chance on Paul disagreeing, so instead of asking him if he could go with her and the class, she merely asked,

"Paul, do you have any plans for Saturday, two weeks from now?"

"Well, I can't say that I do, but you know I always work in the yard Saturday afternoon. Why? What have you got in mind?"

"Actually not anything. I just wanted to see how your schedule was in case I did want to plan something." She lied.

"In that case, if it's anything worthwhile, I'll gladly change my plans. You know that."

Donna was counting on his good nature. So Monday night when she met in the small room with four shaggy-headed little boys, and six bright eyed little girls, she gave each of them a note asking their parents' permission to go on the outing.

Jenny's face lit up like a sunbeam. Donna had never seen her that happy and beautiful before. Donna wanted to pull Jenny to her knee and stroke her long hair. She wanted Jenny to look into her face questioningly as a child does to her mother -- secure, unafraid, protected and loved.

The class began by singing a couple of songs that most five year-olds know, but Jenny didn't open her mouth. Donna didn't want to embarrass her in front of the others, so she made a mental note to ask Jenny about it after class.

Donna had never seen Jenny singing in church either, and it was hard to imagine her not being able to carry a tune.

The project for the week was making a bean-bag, but the first night the class only got them cut out. As she dismissed the children to the sanctuary for a final prayer, Donna motioned for Jenny to come over.

As she took her hand, Donna was looking at Jenny's too-small dress, the scuffed shoes, frayed socks, and the black and blue places on her legs.

Donna had no way of knowing that she received these marks from playing kickball with her brother. Donna pictured Jenny's mother thrashing away at her with a huge black belt while her father stood by silently, afraid for himself. In this reflection Donna forgot how frail Jenny's mother was and in contrast how husky her father was.

"Don't you know the songs we sang tonight? I thought I had picked some that everyone would know."

"No, I don't. You see, I can't read yet."

"But haven't you learned them by hearing other people singing them?"

"Oh, no. I'd rather listen to the piano than the words. The piano is beautiful. Sometimes I dream I can play beautiful songs. Songs that nobody has ever heard."

What innocence! She doesn't realize that she will probably never get the chance to learn to play. Then a conversation came back to Donna. The women who were working on the Bible Study program had been talking about piano lessons here in the church. Now Donna wished she had gone to that fancy restaurant in town that afternoon for lunch, so that she might know if they were indeed planning for a teacher to come to the church building to give lessons to the children.

Donna didn't say anything to Jenny, but she was already picturing Jenny sitting behind the keyboard at the church practicing her scales.

The next morning Donna phoned Mrs. Milligan.

Mrs. Milligan seemed puzzled, but gave Donna the woman's name with just slight hesitation. "You do realize that this woman primarily teaches children?"

Donna dialed Miss. Shoemaker's number before she lost her nerve. Miss Shoemaker was a pleasant woman and Donna pictured her sitting in an old rocking chair, wearing a granny dress and bifocals, devoting all her life to other people's children.

Donna convinced Miss Shoemaker to meet with her and Jenny Wednesday morning.

Donna left for the church about 30 minutes early. She stopped her car in the church parking lot with a jerk and walked swiftly up to the Moore back door. She wanted to get these preliminaries over with before Miss Shoemaker arrived at the church.

When she reached the screen door, Jenny was standing there with a questioning look on her face. "What ya' doing here Mrs. Whitsfield."

"I've come to ask you a favor. Could you walk down to the church with me for a few minutes? I promise it won't take long."

"Well, I'll have ta ask Ma." And with that Jenny disappeared somewhere into the darkness of the small house.

Mrs. Moore was at the door within a minute. "Mrs. Whitsfield. What do you need Jenny for?"

"There is someone coming to the church that I'd like Jenny to meet. I promise I won't keep her long. No more than 30 minutes. I'll even walk her back up the driveway to the door."

"Well, I guess it will be alright, especially, since it is the church she's going to. But no more than 30 minutes. She has a lot of chores to do."

"I promise. She'll have plenty of time to do her chores. Okay, Jenny come on. Let's go." She took Jenny's hand. Donna was so excited that it was difficult to pace herself with the child's shorter stride.

To Donna's chagrin Miss Shoemaker wasn't a day older than 21. She was working her way through college, and had a magnificent diamond on her third finger, left hand. She had been perplexed because Donna wanted to pay for Jenny's lessons, and felt a meeting was necessary to make sure Jenny was serious about taking lessons. Donna assumed that Miss Shoemaker didn't want to tie up her schedule with a student she might lose in a few weeks. But that was not the case.

"Mrs. Whitfield I am very serious about my music, and I want to be sure that this child is not being pushed into something she really has no interest in."

Up until this moment Jenny had not realized that this meeting was about her.

"Me? Piano lessons? You mean, I'm gonna take lessons? You... you're gonna give me lessons? Mrs. Whitfield, is that right?" She was tugging on Donna's sleeve as she jumped up and down.

"Yes, Jenny. If you really want to." Donna answered as she gently unclasped Jenny's hand from her blouse.

Miss Shoemaker needed no further assurance. The only problems left for Donna to handle were Reverend McClure's approval and Jenny's mother's approval. Reverend McClure was delighted to help and gave Donna a key to the sanctuary so she could let Jenny in to practice every day.

That night when Donna told Jenny that Reverend McClure had approved and had given her a key, Jenny said, "Why does the church have to be locked? I thought churches are for people. How can people get in when they want if the doors are locked? They might want to just sit in the quiet, or look at the picture of Jesus on the cross. If the doors stay looked, how can they do that?"

Donna realized that her lack of experience with children was a handicap. "But aren't you glad I'll get to watch you practice every day?" Donna couldn't imagine Jenny not feeling anything for her.

"Of course. I guess Ma wouldn't come over to hear me anyway."

Donna wanted to cry out, "I love you Jenny. It doesn't matter that your mother doesn't care about you. That she beats you. That she won't get a job to dress you like the beautiful little girl you are." But instead, Donna tried to encourage her about her lessons.

Paul was just finishing up his nightly paperwork. As Donna closed the door she smelled a fresh pot of coffee perking. Donna thought, "He's being so understanding about my being gone at night. He usually was so emphatic about me being at home at night, but I guess he realized how much this church program means to me."

Donna poured them both a cup of coffee and carried them into the den. Paul came over and greeted her with the warmest hello kiss she could remember in a long time. "Well, I'll have to go off more often at night, if this is the kind of reception I'll get when I come home."

"Oh, no you won't. This is just a reminder where your place is. I don't want you to get into a habit of this night roaming. I don't know if I can stand being alone seven more nights."

"Well, at least you can see how I feel being left alone every Sunday while you play golf. A taste of your own medicine is not so palatable, huh?"

"One day a week is not the same as ten nights running."

"Oh no? How about 364 Sundays running. That is every Sunday for seven years—364 Sundays."

"Ah ha. Now I've caught you. I went to church with you just about two Sundays ago. Therefore, my golf run has now only been one Sunday running."

"That's not fair. You always manage to come up with some defense."

"You should know by now that I never start an argument I can't win."

They sat together continuing their mock argument until Donna realized that for the first time in several weeks she was enjoying just being with Paul.  For so many nights when they would sit together talking, she had been holding back the thoughts about Jenny-- not sharing Jenny with Paul.   It made her feel deceitful.  But she felt those two worlds could not meet...not yet.

The comfortable atmosphere made her feel this was the time to tell Paul about the note she had sent home with the boys and girls. "Paul, I've invited the boys and girls to spend the Saturday after the study classes up at our cabin."

"Oh, that's great honey.  I was putting off telling you I have to go out of town Thursday week, and I'll probably be gone three or four days.  This will give you something to do."

Consent was what she wanted, but this was not working out the way she had planned.  She wanted Paul to look after the other boys and girls, so that she would have Jenny to herself.  Now she wanted to call the whole thing off.  She didn't want to spend Saturday afternoon with nine wild kids. She wanted to spend Saturday afternoon with Jenny. A calm quiet afternoon, not a wild hiking, keeping up with the kids, counting heads to see that no one was missing afternoon. What could she do?

Paul was turning on the news, so she took the opportunity to take a shower and re-think the situation.

# Chapter 10

Jenny was so excited about the piano lessons she couldn't sleep. She had decided not to tell Fred until she was sure everything was going to work out. So, now, as she lay restlessly, wondering what it would feel like to touch the stiff, cold keys of the piano, she decided that this was the time.

"Fred, are you asleep?"

"If I was, I ain't now."

"I've got to tell you something. I'm going to take piano lessons."

"You're dreaming Jenny. We ain't got no piano. An' more'n that, we ain't got no money to pay for the lessons."

"You're wrong. I'm takin' lessons at the church for free, and I'm usin' the church piano to practice on."

"How'd you manage a thing like that?"

"You know the pretty lady I was tellin' you about that came to the house to invite me to the study classes at church? Well she's payin' for my lessons. And she's comin' over every day to open the church so I can git in to practice."

Fred rolled over, covering his face with his blanket. "I guess Bob's right. Girls have all the breaks. Nobody ever cared if I took piano lessons, or anything else for that matter."

"Who's Bob?"

"Never you mind who he is. He's a friend. I guess my only friend in this whole world."

Jenny wasn't listening any longer, she was dreaming. Dreaming of what it would be like to be Mrs. Whitsfield's little girl. She would probably have her own piano. Probably have her own bedroom. Lots of clothes. Maybe a TV of her own. They would go shopping for toys and fun things, not groceries. She wouldn't have to help in the chicken houses. Mrs. Whitsfield wouldn't have a chicken house.

When Jenny woke the next morning, Fred was already gone. She must have overslept. She would have to hurry to get her chores done, so that she could get over to the church by 1:30 for her first piano lesson. For the first time in her life, Jenny wished for a new dress to wear. She had worn her only good dress to church Sunday and then to the study classes. By the time the classes are over the dress will be worn out.

Nelda had let Jenny sleep late on purpose. She knew the excitement of the piano lessons had been keeping Jenny awake at night. Not because she had checked on her, but because she knew her little girl well enough to know how everything affected her.

Jenny sneaked into the kitchen, half expecting to miss breakfast since she was late.

"Sit down and eat yer breakfast child. It'll be cold in a few minutes."

Jenny obeyed bewildered. As she cleaned her plate, Nelda sat down beside her, "I know how excited you are about these piano lessons; so today why don't you just rest-up. I'll help yer Pa in the chicken house."

Jenny didn't know what to say. She slipped out of her chair and took a step toward her mother, arms outstretched. But before her lips touched the wrinkled skin, Nelda Moore had scooped the dishes off the table and was at the sink depositing them in the sudsy water.

Jenny left the room wondering how she could ever make the time pass until the lesson began.

Nelda was wiping the tears from her face as Mr. Moore came in the back door looking for Jenny.

"I'm gonna help ya today. Jenny's too excited about them lessons."

Mr. Moore smiled, "Well, this will be like old times, with you out there beside me. I hope Jenny stays excited, if it gits you in the chicken house with me."

"Don't go gittin any ideas.  This is for today only. Only."

"One day's better'n none I guess."

# Chapter 11

As usual, Fred met Bob before they went into the old run-down schoolhouse. Bob Lunsford was a couple of years older than Fred. He had been sick when he was in the second grade and had to repeat the second grade the next year when he returned. He was so discouraged because all of his friends were in a higher grade, that he didn't even try to learn anything the first year he came back. Therefore, his third time in the second grade the teacher and principal decided he would have to be promoted. As a consequence, he didn't learn much.

Now that he was in junior high, he was getting promoted just to keep the teachers from having to put up with his pranks more than one year. Lately, his childish pranks were becoming more serious. He had talked a couple of boys into breaking into the school one weekend. They had wrecked several rooms so badly that several doorways and walls had to be replaced. There was no proof of who did it, but everyone knew who it was.

Although Fred was afraid to follow Bob's lead, he did admire his courage, and wanted desperately to be his friend. This particular morning, he just needed someone to talk to. As he detailed his sister's good fortune, Bob's mouth curved up in its usual sneer.

"What'd I tell ya. Girls have all the breaks. Ya never seen no girl fail a grade have ya? And any time there's favors given out, who gits 'em? It's the girls."

More than once, Fred had wanted to run away from home, but he had nowhere to run. He was still a little young to think about earning a living for himself, even if living at home wasn't easy. Today, Fred decided that something had to be done about his life. He wanted a lot from life. He didn't want to turn out like his father, poor, uneducated, and unsuccessful. Bob had some good ideas some times. Fred decided that the next adventure Bob dreamed up would include him.

He didn't have time to change his mind, because Bob was telling him about a little country store they passed every day on the way home from school.

"I've been watchin', and every day the kids git off the bus and fill the place up. That old man will be busy lookin' at all those kids with money, and he won't even notice us if we put a few things in our pockets. We may even git a chance to git to the cash box. He don't have a cash register. Just keeps his money in a metal box right under the counter at the front door. All's we gotta do is be sure and git his attention for just a few minutes, so that one of us can slip our hand in the box and take out a few bills. Not enough so that he will notice."

Fred agreed to help that afternoon on their way home. Maybe he could hide his share of the money until he could use it without anyone noticing. He surely couldn't spend it. His Pa would know if he had money to spend. And he'd be caught right away.

The day dragged slowly for Fred. He'd never done anything dishonest before. His Pa had always said that they were poor, but honest. This idea of the way he was supposed to be stuck in Fred's mind. He remembered it more vividly today than he ever had before.

The bus was so crowded that there were not enough seats for everyone. Bob motioned for Fred to get off, when they pulled up in front of the store. It was tiny. Fred couldn't imagine how the man could possibly earn a living from it. About fifteen or twenty kids got off the bus and piled into the store at the same time. Some were pulling cokes from the cooler, some gathering packs of sweet crackers or candy. Fred wondered how they could afford to stop like this every day and buy something to eat.

Three or four of the kids were searching the cooler for their favorite drink, but couldn't seem to find it. They called the owner over to help them find what they wanted. He had to go into the back room. He knew that while he was gone, some of the kids would put crackers or candy bars in their pockets, but he figured that was part of the overhead for his store.

If he ran the kids off, he would lose a lot of business. His catered to the kids and, therefore, he kept the largest variety of candy and cola of any store in the area. The kids knew it, and that was why they always stopped here rather than at one of the newer stores the bus passed each afternoon. The owner, Mr. Brown, also had set up a couple of booths in the back of the store and a small jukebox. The kids loved it. Not all of them could sit in the two booths, but they piled around them, drinking and eating, $15 maybe $20 worth a day,

Bob took the cue like a professional. As soon as Mr. Brown disappeared behind the door, he was behind the counter, motioning for Fred to lean over the counter so that the other kids couldn't see him. He had the box open, the money in his hand, and was back mingling with the other kids before Mr. Brown got back to the cooler with the supply of cola.

Bob told Fred to pick up a candy bar, and then meet him at the door, but Fred didn't have any money to pay for it. When they reached the counter, Fred told Bob that he didn't have any money. Mr. Brown smiled sympathetically and told him that since this was his first time in the store, the candy was on the house. The two boys bolted out of the store anxious to be alone, so they could divide the money.

They reached a small cluster of trees about a quarter of a mile down the road. Bob decided they had come far enough, so they walked about 20 yards into the thicket and sat down on the softest area of pine straw they could find. As Bob reached into his pocket and pulled out the wad of bills, Fred realized that he was sweating. Bob slowly opened his hand and let the bills fall to the ground. They began laughing and feeling the crumpled money. Suddenly, Fred realized that most at the bills were not one dollar bills as he had expected, but were fives and tens. When they finished with the accounting, they had split $100. Fred was scared.

"Hey, I thought we weren't gonna take all the money. He'll miss this. I thought we were just gonna take a little this time."

"Can I help it if that nut doesn't go to the bank every day? He must've had two or three days' worth of receipts in that box. I just took some off the top. I left plenty. He'll never miss this. I'm tellin' ya. That box was loaded."

"Well, I'd better git home, before my Pa comes lookin' for me."

The boys split up, each heading a separate way home. Fred was uneasy about carryin' so much cash. He wasn't sure how to carry it, or where to put it when he got home.

# Chapter 12

Donna drove up to the church just as Jenny was crossing the drive from her house. Jenny's face was beaming. Donna thought, "Have I really done that? By providing a small gift to her, I changed her life." She was no longer the shy, beaten little girl Donna had seen weeks before. She was so excited that she couldn't be bashful.

These daily meetings were drawing them together emotionally. Donna had become more dependent on Jenny and Jenny was beginning to open up to Donna.

Donna handed Jenny the package she had been half-hiding. "This is just a little something to brighten your day."

"Oh Mrs. Whitsfield, thank you. But I'm not sure I should take a present. My Ma might not like it."

"You just tell your Mother that I don't have a little girl, and I need to give these little dresses to someone. She won't mind, I know she won't." Donna knew Mrs. Moore well enough by now to know that she would let anyone do anything for Jenny. Donna didn't understand her, but her motives didn't matter. At least Donna had been wrong about her abusing Jenny. Donna wrote her off as an unhappy person, rather than a monster. She just wanted Jenny to have the best of everything. So Donna knew that she would let Jenny accept the gifts and continue her piano lessons.

"I'm so excited about the outing tomorrow, I don't know if I can sit long enough to practice today."

"I am too. It doesn't seem like the study classes should be over yet. This has been the fastest two weeks I've ever spent, thanks to you."

"Me? What do you mean?"

"I mean that you have made me very happy. Being with you and sharing a small part of your life has let me see what it would be like to have a little girl like you for my very own."

"You mean you would want a little girl?" Her amazement startled Donna.

"Of course! I would love to have a little girl exactly like you."

"My Ma always says that if it wasn't for me and Fred, she and Pa would be on easy street. I don't think she's too happy she has me."

Every conversation Donna had with Jenny ended the same. She was so unsure of herself, of parental love, of life itself. Donna couldn't bear to hear Jenny sound so unhappy. "Well, you can forget all that tomorrow. If you like, tomorrow we can pretend you are my little girl."

Jenny hugged Donna around the neck and softly whispered in her ear, "I wish I could be your little girl, always."

That innocent statement made Donna determined more than ever to take Jenny from her current family and let her know she was loved. Donna had no idea how to go about it legally, but somehow she would do it.

The next morning when she went to get Jenny, Donna had a plan worked out. "Mrs. Moore, I wonder if I might ask a favor of you? My husband is out of town for the night and I would like to have Jenny spend the night with me so I won't be alone. That is, if it's okay with you." She didn't have to know that Paul had already been away for two nights.

"Well, I'll have to ask Jenny's Pa. But first of all I'll have to ask Jenny."

Jenny had obviously been listening from the kitchen, because she came bursting into the room. "Yes. Yes. Oh, yes. I'd love to. Please, Ma. Please. Let me."

"It's up to yer Pa. I'll go ask him."

"Oh, Mrs.Whitsfield what a wonderful idea. Thank you. Thank you."

"Jenny don't you think we've known each other long enough for you to call me something other than Mrs. Whitsfield? How about Donna?"

"Oh no! My Ma would never stand for me calling you by your first name."

"Well, how about Aunt Donna? That would be okay wouldn't it?" Donna had been surprised by the manners Jenny had when dealing with adults. Mrs. Moore must be trying to do some things right. But why did she act the way she did with Jenny in church? Donna had not seen Mrs. Moore curse even one time at Jenny in their home. What was it about church that made Mrs. Moore so cruel?

Someday, Donna thought, you can call me Mother, not Ma, like you call her. But Mother-- the name of love, devotion, caring.

Mrs. Moore came back in the room, "He says it's okay, but I don't want to put you to no trouble. Now don't do anything special for Jenny."

"Don't you worry. Anything I do for Jenny is because I want to do it. She's a very sweet little girl."

Nelda wasn't too sure of the motives of this strange woman, but she felt it would help Jenny in some way to get closer to her.

They made the rounds to pick up the other children, but because of illness or other conflicts no one else could go except two little boys. The boys evidently had planned this trip together, because they both had their fishing poles and a box of worms. Donna thought "At least I won't have to spend the day babysitting." Maybe it would turn out to be a nice trip after all.

The drive took about half-an-hour, just long enough for the kids to get restless. By the time the car pulled up to the door of the cabin, the boys had their hooks baited and were ready to bail out of the car. They were on the dock fishing before the groceries were unloaded.

"I hope the trip won't bore you, Jenny. I thought at least one little girl would come to keep you company."

"I've got you to keep me company. I don't care about other girls. I'm not much like them anyway. They always have new clothes on, and their hair is always combed. And some of them even paint their fingernails."

"And you don't think much of that, huh?"

"Well, I don't know. I never tried it. It's just that they're different."

"Maybe not. I bought you a new pair of jeans to wear. And if you'd like to try it, I think I have a bottle of fingernail polish in my pocketbook. We could paint your nails."

"Could we? Oh, that would be great!"

It amazed Donna to see how little it took to make Jenny happy. While her nails were drying, Donna started lunch. "Today, I thought we would have pizza. Do you like pizza?"

"I don't know. I never had it. If it's not made with chicken, I probably never will have it."

"No, indeed it isn't. Well I hope you like it because that's all I brought to fix. Tonight when we get home, I'll fix something fancy."

There was no problem with the boys liking the pizza, for, like most kids, they said it was their favorite meal.

After lunch Jenny and Donna took a walk along the bank of the lake. Donna showed her the shad that continually fed there. They stopped and sat down on the bank. Donna began reciting a poem, "Out of the hills of Habersham, Down the valleys of Hall, I hurry aiming to reach the plain, Run the rapid and leap the fall."

"That was pretty. What was it?" Jenny asked.

"That was the first four lines of "Song of the Chattahoochee" written by Sidney Clopton Lanier. Lake Lanier is named for him because of this poem. It describes the counties that surround the lake so well, even though it was written about 70 years before the Corps of Engineers began construction of the dam at Buford in 1950. But it is very appropriate for our lake."

"You're so smart and know so much. Will I ever know that much?"

"Don't worry. By the time you're my age you will know much more than I do. It just seems to happen that way. There is so much more to learn today than there was when I was in school. You'll use computers in school. You'll be able to do research and find out things that I had to go to a library and read a lot of books to find out."

They walked into the woods for a short distance and Donna picked out several wildflowers for her to see. They looked for "little hens" as the old folks called them. Finally, they just sat on the dock and let their feet dangle in the water and talked. Jenny felt so special. Her Ma never had this much time to spend with her. She could learn so much from Aunt Donna.

The boys were no trouble because they were in their own world. The half-dozen fish they caught were just enough to be trouble for Donna, but she couldn't discourage them against taking their prizes home to be praised by their families.

As it turned out, the day was far too short. Before she realized it the sun was setting and she was loading the car with half-empty sacks of uneaten groceries.

She suggested that the kids sing to keep them entertained on the drive home, but unfortunately the only songs Jenny knew were the songs she had learned in the Bible Study class. The boys half-heartedly agreed to sing these. The trip turned out to be an evangelistic chorus.

Jenny was almost out of breath from singing as she helped Donna unload the car. Her face was glowing with excitement.

"Oh, I've never seen anything so beautiful. I never dreamed that anyone could live in a place like this. I thought that all the pictures I had seen were just pretend."

"Well, I guess, some of the pictures are pretend, but this isn't. It's really not all that grand you know."

"It is to me. It's the most beautiful house I've ever seen, and I wish I could live here forever, not just tonight."

Donna resisted the impulse to tell her that somehow she was going to make that possible and suggested that they go and see "her" room.

Donna's preparations had not been wasted. Jenny was as excited about the room as she had been when she first saw the house. A white stuffed cat half-covered the bed with its fluff. She flew to it immediately. She was crying and laughing and rolling on the bed, hugging the cat and saying, "Thank you. Thank you. Oh, thank you."

As Donna closed the curtains, and took out new pajamas, Jenny was examining every item in the room.

"The curtains match the bed cover. I never saw anything so pretty. And it's pink, my very favorite color!"

Donna smiled, "I think it must be most little girls' favorite color. Pink is a girl color, especially if they have beautiful blond hair like you."

"You think my hair is pretty?" Jenny questioned.

"Yes. It's just about the prettiest thing about you, except for your face, and hands and nose," Donna laughed.

"Oh, you're only kiddin'. You're laughin'. I thought you really meant it."

"I do mean it. And wait until you see how it looks after we shampoo and curl it."

The rest of the evening was spent grilling hamburgers, setting her hair, and fixing two double-decker strawberry shortcakes. The hamburgers impressed her, but nowhere near the strawberry shortcakes. As Donna tucked her in bed, long past her bedtime, Jenny looked up and said. "This has been the happiest day in my whole life. I'll never have a happier day. Never!"

"Maybe not a happier day, but you could have more days exactly like this, if you want to."

"I could? How? Ma wouldn't let me to come over and spend the night unless there was a reason."

"We'll worry about that later. Right now let's just think about what good thing you might want for breakfast."

Donna closed the door to her room. It was Jenny's room now. It was as much hers as any child Donna might have had, because Jenny was Donna's daughter. Donna knew that this church was not a place Paul would attend regularly. So, there had to be a reason for her to be so drawn to it. God had put this church in her heart and mind so that she would meet Jenny and care for her. It had to be God's will. Donna had not studied the Bible much in the past few years, but she felt safe in her assumptions that God was leading her.

She heard a car in the driveway. Oh, no! It couldn't be Paul. He said he would be away until Sunday. It isn't Sunday yet. He would ruin everything. Jenny would be distant again with him around. She wouldn't be able to talk to him. How could he do this?

She decided her only alternative was to try and include Paul in her excitement, and maybe, just maybe, he would feel close to Jenny also. She found a smile somewhere within her and ran to the back door.

"Darling. What are you doing home? I didn't expect you until tomorrow."

"Well, I thought I would come home early and surprise my beautiful wife, and see if I could catch her at misbehaving."

"There's no way your surprise can match mine. Now, be quiet and follow me."

She was shaking as she took his hand and guided him up the stairs to the door to the guest bedroom – Jenny's room. He *must* accept her. How could he look at her and not love her?

"Who in the world is that?" Paul's incredulous tone startled Donna.

"You don't recognize her do you? It's Jenny Moore, the little girl from church. She was in my study class and went on the outing today. Since I thought you wouldn't be home tonight, I asked her Mom if she could spend the night with me, so I wouldn't have to be alone again. I've been so lonely these last two nights."

He knelt down at the bed and looked at her so long Donna wondered what he was looking at. Then she saw that he was crying. Could it be that he too was seeing her as his little girl.

"This is the way it would be you know, if our little girl had lived. We'd be tucking her in every night. Only she would be awake to give you a good-night kiss."

He took her arm and guided her out of the room. "No. Donna it's wrong thinking about her as our little girl. Our little girl is dead! Gone! Don't you understand?"

"No she's not. She's lying in there asleep right how. Jenny is MY little girl. I want her; and she needs me. I even think she's beginning to love me. I know I certainly love her. I couldn't love our daughter more. I couldn't."

"But the fact remains that she has parents. No matter how much you want her, you cannot have her, because she already has parents."

"We could do something about that. They aren't fit parents. They can't provide for her. They beat her. We could prove they aren't fit. I know we could. If you would try."

"Donna you don't know what you're saying. I don't even know the little girl and you're asking me to go into court and fight for custody of her. How do you know she would want to live with us?"

"She told me."

"Donna, darling, don't torture yourself. It can never happen."

"It will happen. Somehow it will happen if you don't stop it. If you don't interfere like you did tonight," Donna screamed at him. "You weren't supposed to come home until tomorrow. But you had to come in tonight and ruin my last few hours with Jenny. Why didn't you stay away?"

Suddenly Donna stopped. She couldn't believe what she was saying. She was telling Paul to go away. She had never done that before. She knew him too well. He was the type to leave, if she ever asked him, but he would not be back so quickly. She could never get custody of Jenny if she were divorced.

"Oh, Paul. I'm so sorry. I didn't mean it. I'm sorry. I'm just upset. I love her and I want her to stay here. I haven't felt this alive since I was carrying our child. Don't deny me this."

He put his arms around her and guided her to the bedroom. "All you need is a good night's sleep. You've had a very busy day. You're not accustomed to ten kids all day long."

## Chapter 13

Fred was soothing the marks made by his father's wide black belt with a cold cloth and cursing Jenny's good luck of being out of this house. He still couldn't figure out how his father had found out about the money. He had been very careful to put it in a colored jar and hide the jar under a loose board in the barn.

But his father had found the money and it really didn't matter how he found it. Now all the worrying he had done about how to spend it without arousing suspicion was wasted. His father had said that he was going to keep the money until Fred told him where had gotten it.

Well, it would certainly be a long wait. He would never tell. This lashing was bad enough. If he actually admitted stealing the money, his father would probably beat him to death.

Now he wondered what Jenny was doing. She was probably very happy in that woman's house, getting everything she wanted. Bob was so right. Girls have all the luck. He hated them.

He wondered if he wouldn't be better off running away. He would never be happy here, not with Jenny flouting all her gifts in front of him. If only he knew someone in another city, he could go there and stay until he could find a job.

It was no use; he was stuck. Unless ... *yes*, that was the only answer. If Bob would come up with another way of getting some money, then he would take his share and leave right away. He would go as far as the money would take him. Then let his father see how much work he actually did around this broken-down farm.

For an instant Fred wished that his mother would come into the room and comfort him. But he knew he was just wishing. His mother had never shown any love toward him at all. She acted like he was a burden. She wanted him to be on his own as quickly as possible, so she could use the money she spent on his clothes for Jenny. It didn't matter how a boy looked, but a girl must dress nicely to attract boys.

# Chapter 14

Mrs. Moore was standing outside Fred's door wanting to turn the knob, wanting to feel pity, protectiveness, or love toward him. But she couldn't. His birth had been a financial crisis for her and she would never forgive him for it. They had had to take all their savings out of the bank to pay for his birth and the complications that followed.

He had not been a strong baby and had spent almost a month in the hospital after he was born. The bills that piled up during this period of time took her and Hubert years to repay and was, in large part, the reason they had not been able to remodel the chicken houses or buy better farm equipment.

Instead, she turned and went into the kitchen to finish the dinner dishes. Hubert was sitting with his elbows propped firmly on the table, his head on the palms of his hands.

"Don't you think you were too rough on the boy?" she said as she entered the room.

"No. That's not as bad as a thief deserves."

"But how can you be sure he's one of the boys who stole that money? Nobody knows who done it."

"I know! Mr. Roper said it happened Wednesday afternoon. And that was the afternoon Fred just happened to get off the school bus before his stop. Remember? He was late gettin' here. And that fifty dollars I found couldn't have come from anywhere else. Neither one of us ever has that much money."

"That's true enough. I haven't seen $50 since I married you."

Hubert looked at her in surprise. He knew she wasn't happy, but this was the first time she ever said anything about the way they lived. His old guilt and shame for not providing for her properly hit him square in the face, so he simply left she room, not knowing how to answer her.

He stopped at Fred's door and almost apologetically knocked.

"Come in." Fred growled.

He walked over to where Fred was lying on the bed. "Son, I'm sorry I had to do that. But I thought that somehow over the years you would learn that anything worth having is worth working for. I know you've never done anything bad before, but you could get put in jail for something like this."

"You're willing to say I'm guilty without giving me a chance to say my piece. A fine father you are. You'll probably turn me in."

"No. I won't. You're my son. And if I can help it, no son of mine will ever go to jail. But you ain't gonna keep the money either. You and me are gonna put it back."

"What do you mean, put it back? I sweated for that money. Just as much as if I'd worked for it."

"So you're admittin' it. You did take it. Where's the rest of it? Roper said $100 was taken. You've only got $50. Where's the rest?"

"I spent it." Fred spit back at his father.

"You couldn't. I'd've known if you had. You ain't got nothin' new."

"That's the only answer you're getting from me."

"Well, never mind. You're still gonna return what you have. And you're gonna write a note sayin' that you're sorry you done it."

"That's the same as turnin' me over to the cops. They'll come get me."

"No, they won't. You don't have to sign the note. That's the way it's gonna be. Now you just start writtin' that note, 'cause tomorrow we're gonna return that dough."

He walked out of the room satisfied that the matter was over.

Fred began writing the note between curses at Jenny's good fortune and momentary pauses to put another cool cloth on his back. For the life of him, he couldn't imagine how they would put the money back.

The night proved to be long and uncomfortable for Fred. But morning finally came, and with it a deadening of pain in the belt marks on his back and a stirring of fear in his stomach.

Breakfast was not the same without Jenny chattering away at the table. The strain the three of them shared was so intense none dared speak.

After the ordeal was over, Mr. Moore told Fred to go get the letter he had written. He checked it to make sure it sounded sufficiently apologetic and put it and the $50 in an envelope.

The chores in the chicken house came first. And the weather was beginning to get cold enough now that they must use heaters to keep the chickens warm. He and Fred went out to feed the chickens and check the temperature to make sure the heaters were working properly.

The coops needed cleaning and Fred volunteered to do it as a means of postponing the trip he and his father were going to make. But Mr. Moore was anxious to go while everyone else was in church.  So they hurried with their duties and got in the truck for their short but unnerving ride.

As they neared the store, Mr. Moore told Fred to see if any familiar cars were behind them.  He didn't want anyone to see them stop in front of the store.

He turned the truck slowly onto the gravel parking area in front of the store, pulled up the handbrake, but left the motor running.

"Fred, now you just jump out and slip this envelope under the door and no one will ever know we've been here."

Fred obeyed his father with a good deal of questioning.  He had no choice for now.

Just as Hubert pulled the truck back onto the highway a small red car made a left turn in front of him into the store's parking area.  The man waved friendly to the truck rather than its occupants, since he had never seen the driver before and the boy looked only vaguely familiar.

"That's the owner. Pa that's the owner! He'll remember me. And when he finds that note and money he'll send the police after me."

"Now you've got no cause to start worryin'. He don't even know you and he probably didn't see you anyway."

But Fred knew he would remember. Remember that he had only been in his store once -- the day his money was stolen. He wouldn't be satisfied with half the money. He'd want the rest of it and he would come looking for Fred to get it.

Now, more than ever before, Fred knew he had to get away. If he didn't, he would go to jail.

# Chapter 15

It was a perfect morning for rising early. The sun flooded each room with its warmth as Jenny lay in bed watching its rays bounce off the dresser mirror and glance on the picture of two little blond girls dressed in long pink frilly dresses, one carrying a pink parasol and the other carrying a white kitten. She snuggled with the white stuffed kitten that had been on her bed last night.

Yes, it was her bed and she knew she could sleep in it whenever she wanted. She felt love from Aunt Donna. The mother's love she had been denied for so many years. She wished Donna was her mother, but she knew she couldn't be. She could love her and spend some nights with her, but her real mother would never let her live with Donna.

As she dreamily closed her eyes to imagine waking in this beautiful room every morning, the door partially opened and Donna peeked through the crack.

"Oh, God, why can't I have her? I love her more than her own mother. Why can't she wake in my house every morning? Why is she doomed to live in the poverty of her parents?"

"Aunt Donna?"

Startled, Donna opened the door and stepped in, "Good morning. How's my little girl this morning?"

"I wish I was. Am I bad for saying that?"

"No, darling. You're not bad. If you really want it. If you could really be happy with us..."

"Who is us?"

"Me and Paul, my husband. You are going to meet him just as soon as you brush your hair and put on your robe. He's waiting to meet you."

"But I thought he wasn't here."

"He wasn't. He came in late last night and he's dying to meet you."

"No. He'll be mad 'cause I'm here."

"Of course he won't. He came in and kissed you in your sleep last night. He's not mad. He's glad you're here."

"He kissed me? I never had a man kiss me before. My own Pa never kissed me. Paul really must like me. Let's go!"

She jumped out of bed, brushed her hair and let Donna help her slip her robe on. "What are we having for breakfast?"

"How does French toast and sausage sound?"

"I never had that kind of toast before, but I like sausage."

"Fine. Then let's go meet Paul and, while you're visiting I'll finish breakfast."

Paul was dressed and waiting for them at the kitchen table.

"Well, hello Jenny. Donna didn't exaggerate. You are a beautiful girl. Did you sleep well?"

"It was perfect! Gee, you're handsome. Aunt Donna didn't tell me that."

Paul gave Donna a suspicious look.

"I told her to call me Aunt Donna, because Mrs. Whitsfield sounds too formal for our special relationship."

He decided not to make an issue over it. "Well, if you're Aunt Donna, I guess I must be Uncle Paul. Okay, little Jenny?"

Jenny blushed with happiness, "Aunt Donna told me that you gave me a kiss while I was sleeping last night. Can I give you one now?"

Paul stumbled for words, but Jenny didn't wait for an answer. She threw her arms around his neck and kissed him so warmly on the cheek, with all the love she had been holding in her all her life, that he couldn't have refused if it had been his intention.

The rest of breakfast was like something Donna had dreamed of for years. They were like a real family. Jenny entertained them with her constant chatter about how pretty everything was, and how good the food was, and most of all, how great it was that she didn't have to hear the chickens.

It was understood that Paul would be going to church with them. And Donna was determined to show him how wonderful it would be to attend church as a family.

They looked for Mrs. Moore but could not see her. Donna was glad that Jenny would be able to sit with her and Paul, and was proud at the way Jenny looked in the new outfit she had bought for her.

Jenny began looking around for her mother, "I wonder where she is. She never missed a Sunday before. Maybe she's sick. "I'd better go home."

"Now Jenny, everything's all right, don't worry. We would have heard if your Mother was sick. Let's sit here."

Jenny sat down obediently. In fact, she sat motionless throughout the entire service, but Donna could tell she was thinking about her mother. That she couldn't wait for the service to be over so that she could rush home to make sure everything was okay.

She had seemed so happy this morning. Donna thought, maybe I'm wrong to think she could ever love us. No. I'm not wrong. How silly of me to think such a thing. It will just take a little more time. That's all. She needs time.

Paul and Donna walked Jenny to her house after the service was over. Before they reached the steps, Jenny was inside calling to her mother.

"Evidently you misjudged Jenny's feelings for her mother. She seems very concerned."

"Just because she doesn't want anything bad to happen to her doesn't mean that she would choose to live with her as opposed to living with me."

"Oh, excuse me. I thought she would be living with both of us. Not just you."

Jenny was holding the door open. "She's okay. They just had an errand to run this morning. She didn't even feel bad at all. Uncle Paul come in."

Nelda seemed a little disturbed, but was courteous. She thanked them for taking care of Jenny.

Donna wondered if Mrs. Moore could sense what she was thinking about doing. Of course not! There was no way she could know that she wanted to take Jenny from her.

Paul extended his hand to Mrs. Moore.

"I sure do appreciate you bringing Jenny home Mr. Whitsfield, but I thought you were away last night." She said as she looked at Paul.

Paul cast a cautious g1ance at Donna. "I was supposed to be. I thought I would surprise Donna by coming home early. But she had a bigger surprise for me."

"I hope that Jenny didn't put you out."

"No. I was very glad Donna had someone to visit with her while I was away. We both love children." For some reason he felt relaxed with this woman. She stood before him in a faded brown dress and worn out loafers. Her hair was pulled back and fastened with a rubber band at the nape of her neck. A few strands of stubborn brown hair dangled at the side of her face. She wore no makeup. Maybe this lack of artificial paint was the thing that made her seem so honest, so open. Paul found himself telling her about their dead daughter.

"I never thought that I would be able to tell another living person about her. We wanted her as badly as any parents want their first child, maybe more. Her death tore us up. I guess neither of us has gotten over her.

Nelda smiled as if she understood. But Paul knew that no one could understand the grief of losing a child unless it happened to them. No one could understand the emptiness life held. The months when eating was a ritual you practiced out of habit. Sleeping was a seldom blessing. Laughing was nonexistent. Life itself was a burden.

Somehow it seemed easier now. Now that he had said all the words. Was it Nelda that had brought all of this out of him? Or was it Jenny?

Mrs. Moore excused herself to get them some coffee.

Paul suddenly realized that he and Mrs. Moore had been alone. Where had Donna and Jenny disappeared?

Paul gazed around the room in disbelief. The outside of the house had been a shock to him, but the inside almost reminded him of some of the slum houses he had seen on the often-remembered field trips in college, There was a wood-burning stove in the center of one wall. The rough-hewn walls were painted with a thin coat of pink paint and there were distinct cracks between the boards, letting in both daylight and cold air. The linoleum rug was frayed on the edges and the wine and the brown colored design had faded to a dirt-and mud color. There was a red vinyl sofa on the inside wall next to the kitchen and opposite it under two long curtainless windows was a small-screened black and white TV. The only light in the room came from a single naked bulb hanging from the ceiling in the center of the room. And although it must have been 150 watts, the room was dark and dreary. Paul wondered why the bright sunlight did not help to brighten the room.

 For the first time since Donna had told him about Jenny, he understood why she felt sorry for her. He felt an immediate desire to help her too. But he knew down deep inside where all the pains of life are kept secret from others, that there was nothing he could do. You just can't interfere in other people's lives. He must convince Donna of that.

 Jenny and Donna came back into the room from the direction of Jenny's bedroom and Paul was stricken with the happiness between them. They were holding hands and Jenny was whispering something in Donna's ear. They both laughed out loud. The first genuine happy laugh Donna had had in five years.

 Mrs. Moore must have noticed a change in Jenny. Must have sensed that her daughter and Donna were sharing something personal because she immediately rushed Jenny out of the room.

"Isn't she precious, Paul?" Donna beamed.

"Yeah. She's quite a little doll."

"I knew you'd love her once you were around her for a while."

"Let' not talk about it now. This is not the place."

They gulped their coffee and left with the excuse that they knew they were interfering with the Moore'' Sunday meal,

Looking out the window of the car, Donna saw beauty in the pines, mimosas and magnolias that lined the curving highway. She was amazed how beautiful the country looked to her now. The numerous farms they passed seemed to have grown greener since the last time she was on this road. The black top caught the sun's bouncing rays and threw them back at the car like hundreds of diamonds. Donna felt good and she wanted to share her feelings with Paul. He must see her reasoning. He must agree to her plan.

Paul sat quietly feeling the excitement from Donna. He didn't know what she had in mind, but he did know that their plans could not include Jenny. He dreaded the talk they must have and made certain that he would not be the one to begin any such conversation. The trip home seemed endless, but yet he didn't really want it to end. He knew where it would take place. They would get home and Donna would finish lunch. They would eat quietly and then when they were settled in the den with their second cup of coffee, she would begin. It would end in tears, but he would have to ready himself for this. Maybe she did it on purpose, he didn't know. `She always got her way after the tears. But one thing was certain; today she would not.

# Chapter 16

Nelda watched Jenny's face during lunch and she couldn't remember it ever being so beautiful. She was happy. It showed in her eyes. She couldn't even keep from smiling during the solemn meal.

Fred and Hubert said nothing, their own problems keeping them occupied. Fred ate little which was unusual for him. Nelda sometimes thought he would eat everything stored in her kitchen if he were let loose long enough.

Nelda wondered what had happened at the store. They both had been so quiet when they came in. But she knew Hubert world tell her when the time was right. More importantly, she wanted to find out what Jenny thought of her new benefactress. So as they cleared the table she casually asked. "Did you have a good time yesterday?"

"It was wonderful; I never had so much fun. I didn't want it to end."

Nelda wanted to ask more. To get answers about the intimate things that might have taken place between her little girl and that strange woman. She wanted to ask, but was afraid of the answers. Jenny had taken up with Mrs. Whitsfield so eagerly it half-scared Nelda to think about it. She could almost see the kind of life Jenny world live if she belonged to these people. And she could see the change in Jenny's attitude. She wanted all this for her child. But she wanted to share Jenny's success in life; she didn't want all the good things to happen to Jenny in someone else's home.

Hubert came in and closed the kitchen door. "Jenny, go outside for a while. I want to talk to your Ma."

"Maybe you'd better change that new dress first. You don't want to mess it up." Nelda cautioned.

"Okay. But I bet if I lived with Aunt Donna "I'd have lots of new dresses to wear."

"Aunt Donna? Who is that? Hubert was getting agitated at this delay."

"That's Mrs. Whitsfield. She didn't think that name was proper, since we're so close." Jenny was enjoying the uneasiness she could feel in her parents. For the first time she could tell that they cared for her by the way they kept glancing at each other, and by the look in their eyes.

"She's no relative and I don't want to hear ya call her that again."

Jenny left the room sulking. He had no right to tell her that. She could call Donna aunt if she wanted to. He had no right. No right at all. He didn't love her.

Mr. Moore turned to Nelda. "We sure don't need any problems from Jenny. We've got enough with Fred. He saw the owner of the store as we were pulling out on the highway. Thinks the guy will recognize him."

"Oh no. What's this gonna do to Jenny?"

"Jenny? What do you mean? What's this gonna do to Fred? If they catch him, he'll go to jail."

"Well, maybe he deserves it. He did take the money. Jenny didn't do anything, but she'll have to pay for it. Everyone will think of Fred when they see her. She'll never have a chance to get out of this place."

She was getting hysterical. Hubert hadn't seen her like this in a long time. She used to have spunk; used to care enough about things to get upset. In the past 20 years, she just ignored life, never seemed to notice him or their children. His love for her was strangely rekindled as he watched her. He knew that she really did care about life. Now he could go to her, be the husband he had not been for years.

"Nell, honey, we can work things out together." He put his arms around her and she let him hold her, protect her for just a few minutes.

Fred had been sitting on the workbench beside the back door and heard the conversation between his parents. He never felt less loved than he did at this moment. He didn't think his Mother loved him very much, but he couldn't believe she would want him to go to jail. She was only interested in protecting Jenny. Bob had been right again. "That does it," he thought. "Now I've got to get enough money to get away from here. I guess I can't hurt anybody if I'm not around."

Monday morning Fred found Bob as soon as he got to school. Bob wasn't very receptive to Fred's plan. His mischief had always been boyish pranks to him. He never considered anything he had done as criminal until the day he wanted to prove himself do Fred and suggested taking the money from the grocery store. The truth was, he still felt uncomfortable about the money and had his share hidden with no intention of ever spending it.

Fred had always looked up to him. Made him feel important and he didn't want Fred to think he was afraid. "I'll have to think about it for a while."

"If you don't want to, just say so." Fred was afraid Bob didn't think he had been brave enough in their previous venture together. He never doubted Bob's bravery.

"Hey! It's not that. It's just that I'm tryin' to think of a place with enough money to make it worthwhile."

"I know just the place. You know that all night gas station on Highway 51? It's close enough for me to walk to. We could meet there Saturday night. They're sure to have some money and not many customers, if we wait until about midnight."

"I don't know Fred. How'd we go about gettin him to give us the money?"

"You've got a gun haven't ya?"

"No, I don't."

"Well, yer Pa's got a shotgun I bet. We can use it."

Bob was beginning to get nervous, but he didn't want to lose Fred's admiration. "I've never seen you like this. What's your hurry? You must have a good reason."

"The best. I'm leaving town after we get the money. I'll hitch a ride to Atlanta and catch a bus or train from there."

"You can't go off by yourself like that!"

"Why don't you come with me? Maybe we could stay in Atlanta. Most of the kids there share rooms. We'd fit right in."

"I don't know. My Pa'd skin me if he ever found me."

"He'd never find you there. You sure are actin' funny. You've been tellin' me that's exactly what you'd like to do."

"Sure. It is. Okay, Saturday night's the night."

# Chapter 17

The day was gray and cold, but the weather didn't bother Donna. Sunday held a special meaning for her now, and nothing could dampen her spirits. She was going to see Jenny. They would talk, and then she would ask Mrs. Moore to let Jenny spend the night with her. She had it all planned. There would be no reason for refusal. She and Paul had had their 'talk' last Sunday. It had ended with her in tears, but for the first time Paul had not given in. He said he could easily love Jenny, but that they were not going to interfere in the child's life. It could only cause pain. Donna decided not to pursue it any further, but she hadn't given up. Somehow she would get her way. It might take longer than she had planned but she would eventually have Jenny living in her house.

As she walked in the church she wondered what the special occasion was. Every pew in the always half-empty church was filled. It must be something pretty special to get all these people out. She had never seen some of these people before in her eleven months of visiting this church. Strange that she couldn't seem to find Jenny. She finally saw a vacant space near the front between Mrs. Milligan and some woman she had never seen. She hesitated because she never liked walking in front of the congregation to get a seat. She sensed the other women looking her over. But there was really no choice. She must make the walk and her delay was only making it worse.

She scanned each pew as she walked down the aisle, but Jenny wasn't there. What if something were wrong with her. Donna couldn't stand the thought. She tried to put it out of her mind.

When Mrs. Milligan realized that it was Donna who was squeezing in beside her, she was delighted at the prospect of gossiping about the county's most scandalous news in 20 years. Not since the time when she was a young girl and her best friend's suitor had been found with another man's wife and had been shot five times. Mrs. Milligan had insisted that she had tried to warn her "friend" about the kind of man she was planning to marry, but the friend took no heed. And after it was all over, she lost her friend because the poor woman refused to admit that she had been a poor judge of character.

Now Mrs. Milligan was spurred on with the prospect of news-telling. She was positive that Donna had not heard the news because she lived on the other side of town. Although the radio had reported what had happened, it could not give the names of the boys because they were under age. She started with a fake concerned look on her face.

"I guess you heard about Fred Moore and that friend of his?'

"Heard what?" Donna started.

"I don't know if you noticed, but Mrs. Moore and that nasty child of hers are not here today. Afraid or ashamed to show their faces, I guess. Well, anyway, it seems that last right Fred and Bob decided to get their hands on some money. So Bob took his father's gun and they met at the all-night station on Highway 51 sometime after midnight. But that Roger Martin was ready for any kind of foolishness ever since he was robbed about two years ago. Almost wiped him out. So he bought himself a gun."

Donna was getting so impatient she almost shouted for Mrs. Milligan to continue. Just at that moment the Minister of Music stepped up to the podium and asked the congregation to stand for the Doxology. Donna could barely make the sounds pass her vocal cords to form the words. "Praise God from whom all blessings flow..." She wanted to run out the front door screaming. Run for Jenny. Protect her. Mrs. Milligan's voice rose high above everyone's in the area where Donna was standing. How could this woman at one moment be gloating over telling bad news and in the next, sing praises to God?

Finally the prayer was over and they were sitting down for announcements. Now she could prompt Mrs. Milligan to finish her explanations. She took no prompting. "Anyway, what I was saying was that these two <u>hoodlums</u> went to poor old Martin's station with the intention of robbing him. Only when he saw them coming with that shotgun, he drew his pistol. When they demanded his money he fired at them."

Donna was shaking. Even though she had no love for Fred. In fact, she'd only seen him a couple of times. She felt compassion for him. She could understand what might drive him to do this. And now he was probably shot, maybe even dead. No. Wait a minute. Mrs. Milligan wasn't saying that. "He got off one shot before that Bob shot him, and it was a perfect hit. Got Bob right in the heart. But, of course, poor old Roger Martin got hit too. Only it didn't kill him. They don't know how bad it is now. But that Moore kid's in jail. Right where he belongs too, if you ask me."

Jail? How could that be? What would happen to Jenny? This could ruin her life. The thoughts came one after the other, flashing. The sermon dragged on, "Come unto Him, and ah, He will forgive, ah, your sins, ah."

Fred's sins? Mrs. Moore's sins? Indeed, her own sins? "Oh God, could You forgive all those sins? The sins she knew she committed, and those deeply hidden sins she had forgotten, or tried to forget. God, could you forgive all that? For the first time she could remember, Donna called on God to help her, not for herself, but for Jenny and Fred. She must help both of them.

"God if you will help me to help them, I will do what's best for them, not me. I'll try to separate my own feelings. I love Jenny, but I'll try to think of her needs and not mine." Her prayer was sincere; she was sweating; her palms were wet; she was shaking. And then at once she felt a calm overcoming her. She wasn't anxious anymore.

There was a light rain falling when she had entered church earlier; now the sky ominously foretold that the rain would soon be sleet, and maybe even later, snow. No small groups were forming outside as they usually did. Everyone was rushing to their cars to go home before the roads became impassable.

# Chapter 18

There was no Sunday meal being prepared in the Moore kitchen that morning. Nelda was sitting numb in her robe at the kitchen table. She had barely moved from her chair all morning. With her finger she was tracing each nick in the white painted table. She noticed the drabness in her kitchen as if for the first time. Symbolic of the drabness in her life. And now Jenny's fate was to be almost a replica of her own. She would remain in these unhappy surroundings; or move to others like them. Despite everything Nelda had done for her, Jenny would ultimately suffer, because of a man, or a man-child, Fred.

She could still hear the sirens blaring as the police cars careened into the yard, scaring the chickens half to death. The red lights flashing, the shouts, the pounding on the door and Fred hand-cuffed sitting in the back seat of the police car, head down, hair in his eyes. He would not look up at them; he wouldn't explain what had happened. And Hubert was dragged down to the police station with them. She remembered them saying that a man had been shot and another boy, in fact a friend of Fred's, had been killed. She still couldn't understand it all. What did all that have to do with Fred? He wasn't the kind of boy to be involved in anything like that. No, she couldn't believe he would ever do anything dishonest. But still he was in jail and Hubert was worried.

When he had finally come in sometime during the hours of the morning, Hubert told her everything that had happened. Fred had encouraged Bob to help him rob the station so he could get some money for his adventure to Atlanta. Bob had been carrying his father's shotgun just for show. But he had been the one that the station owner shot. Bob must have been frightened when he saw Roger Martin draw his gun out from under the counter, so he fired without warning Fred.

She listened quietly without uttering a word. She had little sympathy for Fred, but she knew she could not let Hubert know her feelings. Instead, she chose to stay in the kitchen at the table the remainder of the night. Hubert went out to the chicken house to work out his anguish. They had both kept at their separate sorrowing until now when Jenny came running in the room.

"Ma where's Fred? Aren't we gonna be late for church? When's breakfast?"

For once Nelda was glad for her daughter's habit of asking more than one question at a time. So she evaded the first question.

"We are not going to church today. I didn't feel well and accidentally overslept."

Jenny immediately noticed the change in her mother's voice. She was speaking slowly, distinctly, somehow like she had never heard her speak before. She sounded almost like Aunt Donna. The way she pronounced the words; she was not slurring them together as she usually did. More importantly she did not sound aggravated at Jenny like she usually did.

"Well, when will we eat?" She repeated the question since her mother had not answered it. By this time, she had forgotten about Fred. He was very seldom on her mind anyway.

The idea of cooking now was more than Nelda could handle. Before she could think of an answer, someone knocked on the front door. "Jenny, go answer the door."

Jenny ran to open the door and squealed with delight when she saw Donna standing there. "Oh, I thought I wouldn't get to see you today. Ma's sick and slept late, so we didn't make it to church."

Donna realized that Jenny didn't know anything about Fred, so she didn't mention him. "Is your Mother up now? I'd like to speak with her."

"Yes. She's in the kitchen. I'll show you."

"No, why don't you go put on a pretty dress and let me find her?" It seemed that Jenny was happy to do anything Donna asked. She skipped off to her room and Donna went into the kitchen to find Nelda.

"I heard the terrible news at church. I just wanted to see if I could help."

"I don't think so. We don't know what we are going to do ourselves. We haven't had a chance to talk yet. And with Jenny around wanting to eat, she'll be in the way all day and I don't know when we'll get a chance."

"Maybe I can help after all. How about letting Jenny spend the day with me. Lunch will be ready by the time I drive us home. That way you and Mr. Moore can have the whole day to do your planning. Better yet. Let her spend the night. I'll bring her back after she practices her piano tomorrow. Okay?"

"Well, I guess it would be better if we had time to be alone and figure things out. I don't want Jenny to know about Fred. It's bad enough having everyone talking about us behind our backs, but I don't think I can stand them pointing at Jenny."

She didn't bother to get permission from Mr. Moore. Jenny packed a brown paper bag with her pajamas and clothes for the next day and they were off.

# Chapter 19

Sitting in church that Sunday morning, Donna realized that she could not force herself on Jenny. She could not rush things. She must let things happen naturally. She could love Jenny and let the circumstances work themselves out. Her only purpose was to try and make Jenny happy.

Now, weeks later, it seemed that things had worked out better than she could have hoped. Jenny was living with her and Paul, even though it wasn't a permanent arrangement. As the days slipped by, Donna tried to get in touch with Mrs. Moore to see when she wanted Jenny to come home, but Mrs. Moore kept finding excuses for letting Jenny stay with Donna. The trial date had not even been set yet, and it looked like it could be months before Fred would actually have to go on trial.

The court had appointed a Public Defender for Fred, but Donna wondered how hard he would try to get Fred acquitted.

Fred did look guilty, but his attorney would have to understand his motives. He would have to go into Fred's home, overhear private conversations, see the conditions under which he was brought up. Then, maybe, he could understand why Fred needed an escape. But this man wouldn't know this; he probably wouldn't care. How many other cases would he be working on? Donna was determined not to let her concern for Fred ruin her relationship with Jenny. She decided to let those problems alone and devote all her time to Jenny.

And Jenny did seem happy. She didn't ask about her family, didn't even ask when she would be going home. It was like she was afraid to mention her stay. Afraid that a mention of it would break a spell and she could awaken and find that she had been dreaming. So they played their roles--Donna the devoted mother, and Jenny the perfect daughter. Paul even got into the act. He played a very good father. Made sure Jenny ate her vegetables, drank all her milk. He worried about cavities, playing out in the cold and what he would do when she went back home. This he didn't mention to Donna. He couldn't bring himself to talk about their being childless again. Jenny seemed so much like their daughter and her mother didn't seem anxious to get her back.

The days had melted into weeks, and Paul and Donna were thinking about how they would handle Christmas. Their usual visit to parents' homes would be very touchy with Jenny along. They had always spent Christmas with Donna's family, since his parents went to his brother's house in Naples, Florida. He didn't feel neglected that his parents wanted to get to a warm climate during the winter. They usually stayed a month with his brother and his wife. They had 3 children and waking Christmas morning with children in the room was much more exciting than it would have been with him and Donna.

Donna's family would gather at her parent's home with her brother and sister and their five children. It was a real family Christmas. Many times they would have snow during Christmas week. Donna's sister was a piano teacher and after the mid-day meal always played Christmas carols while the whole family attempted to sing along. Donna was the only one who had formal voice training and she had kept the family in tune as much as one person could.

Paul wasn't sure how Donna's family would accept them bringing Jenny home with them, especially since she had her own family. There would be lots of questions. Questions he frankly didn't want to answer because he couldn't really accept what they were doing himself.

One night as they were sitting in the den, Donna knitting Jenny a sweater, Paul finishing the paper, the doorbell rang. Jenny ran to see who it was. She returned arm-in-arm with a man neither Donna nor Paul had ever seen.

"I'm Jenny's grandfather." He removed his hat and showed white hair to match his white moustache.

"We didn't know Jenny had any grandparents."

"I'm the only one left. I've never seen Jenny. Her father and I never hit it off; so I've never been here. When I read about Fred in the paper, I thought perhaps I might be better qualified to defend him. I waited to see if Nell would call and ask me to come. But when she didn't, I decided that it was time to swallow my pride and came anyway. Fred needs me too bad."

Jenny had been listening to him so intently she realized something was wrong with Fred. "Why does Fred need you? Is he hurt?"

"He's hurt in a way. In fact, it may be the worst kind of hurt a person could have. But don't you worry. I'm going to help him."

Jenny loved her grandfather from the first minute she saw him. She had been sitting in his lap as she had so often sat in Paul's, and when he finished telling her about Fred she hugged him. And to her delight he hugged her back.

"Where are you staying?" she wanted do know.

"At your house. Don't you want to come back with me? Your mother told me where you were and she sure does miss you."

Donna's heart stopped. He couldn't come in from out of the past and just take his granddaughter that he's never seen. It wasn't his place. Jenny belonged to her and Paul. She had prayed for God to show her the way and to let her help this family. And He had shown her the way. He placed Jenny in her home. This old man had no right. He didn't understand the situation at Jenny's house. But Donna could see Jenny really wanted to go with him.

"I went over to the Moore's yesterday and Nelda asked me to keep Jenny a little while longer." Maybe the familiarity of using Nelda's first name would make him think that she and Nelda were close friends.

"That was before I arrived. A family should be together in bad times. Having Jenny around will make us all feel better." Obviously he had no idea of the life Jenny had led. Maybe he would see when he got Jenny and her mother together.

Donna thought Jenny has forgotten all she had given her—their love and their home. She was already packing her bag. A pink overnight bag that Donna had bought for her on one of their frequent shopping sprees. Every item she put in the bag was something Paul and Donna had given her. Donna wanted to cry, to pull everything out and remind Jenny that she wouldn't have any of this if it hadn't been for them. But Jenny was beyond reaching. Her eyes were sparkling with the excitement of going home. Donna's mind cried, "This has been more of a home in these few weeks, than that other place where you've had no love for years." But then she realized that it didn't matter to Jenny.

Jenny loves her mother and father, and that was enough to make up for the lack of love on their part. Maybe she had been waiting all these weeks for someone to come and get her. Donna wanted that kind of love from Jenny, or a child of her own. A love that would never die, regardless of the faults of the people involved. A loyal love, innocent love. It was the kind of love God gives us. Donna thought, "Maybe I need to look to God for that kind of love."

Donna kissed her and Jenny threw her arms around Donna's neck as if she were sorry for a split-second. But then she grabbed her grandfather's hand and they left.

Jenny was gone.

## Chapter 20

In order to have something else to do for a few Sundays, Donna made the extra effort to get up early enough to attend the 'young married women's classes'. The class began with a role call, a count of the number of attendees with Bibles, how many staying for church, and how many tithing. Then there was a lengthy discussion of who was not present and much discussion of why they were absent.

It was assumed that they had not been living a proper Christian life and they were dismissed with much condescending talk of praying for them. Then there was a discussion of what everyone was wearing and what everyone did the night before. Finally, there was a hurried reading of the scripture, a pause, a summary of the lesson shortened out of proportion, then a hurried embarrassed prayer and the class was dismissed with everyone feeling quite good about themselves for being there.  The discussion on the walk to the Sanctuary covered everyone who had not been discussed in the classroom.

Donna thought, "This is not for me." She was tired of the Sunday school gossip.  I feel more like I've been worshiping when I take a long drive through the country, or when I spend the day on the lake. "No thank you.  I don't need that."  There were several other classes--the adult women's class, the young married couple's class, the lamplighter's class and God and his disciples.  But Donna knew they were all as phony as the one she had chosen today.  There was simply no reason to waste her time attending one of these classes.

Today, Donna was surprised to find a new face behind the pulpit. She had not been to church in several weeks.  She decided Paul was right.  She must leave well enough alone.

The new man was over six feet tall, slender and wearing a very self-assured air about him.  She heard Reverend McClure introduce him as the new youth minister,

It was true that the church had grown so rapidly in the last nine months that the youth could profit from some direct leadership. This Craig Bennett seemed to be fully capable of handling any problems the youth of the church could stir up.

He was inviting all the boys and girls under age 13 to join him down in the Sunday school rooms. He said they would have their own church service while the adults had their's.

Maybe this new man offered some hope for the young people. He certainly wasn't orthodox. His face was animated with something Donna had never seen before in a preacher. He was young and muscular. The young girls sure weren't wasting time following him to the basement classrooms.

Donna's heart stopped. How will I ever get to see Jenny if she's down there every Sunday? She was still trembling as she slid behind the wheel of the car for the lonesome journey home.

There was no need to return to this church again. She gained no comfort from God here.

When Paul came home, he found Donna sitting at the kitchen table staring at the wall. The door had been left open, but her mind was closed to the outside world.

At first he panicked when she wouldn't answer him, and then he remembered all those other days when he would come home from work and find her like this. Those days after their baby had died. He pulled her to her feet add put his arms around her. Gently, he guided her to the bed and for the next two days he fed her warm milk, hot soups and sat next to her, holding her hand and kissing her on the forehead frequently. Finally his warmth and closeness made her open up again to the pain of another loss and release the pain in a storm of tears.

# Chapter 21

Donna couldn't bring herself to keep going to the little church Sunday after Sunday being ignored by Jenny. She had sought out this church because she had been looking for a real religion. One where people were honest with themselves and God. But she had found this little church to be a replica of the other churches she had attended. She didn't know of a person in the church who was really interested in being Christ-like. Not even herself. That was the worst thing. She had expected this church to do something for her. To give her life some kind of meaning. And when she discovered Jenny and her problems, she had thought that maybe Jenny was the answer. But it had just been a dream. A non-reality like all the other non-realities she had experienced all her life.

Things she was supposed to feel, the greatest events of her life had somehow let her down. Her graduation from college was supposed to be a big day. A step into the future. But for her it was somehow anti-climactic. Her wedding day, supposedly the most cherished day in every girl's life was for her just a formality for her parents' sake. She had been Paul's wife in her mind for many months before the ceremony. Then the birth of her child. This was going to be something real, she knew it. This would give her the feeling of accomplishment she had looked for all her life. But then the baby died. It was as if God were saying "No, you may not find happiness on earth. Look for it later." She had been looking for it. Searching for a church that would not say to her, "This is it. You will suffer in this life, but be rewarded in the next."

Since Jenny was rejecting her, she must now try to find another church. There was no easy way to choose another church. Evidently the things she had looked for before were not important. She decided that after Christmas she would go to First Baptist, because it was much closer to her home.

Donna and Paul made plans to visit Greenville for Christmas. Donna's mother was so excited. She had not seen her daughter in several months and was eager for the closeness they had always shared. The whole family would be there. Maybe it would be a Christmas like old times.

As it turned out, Christmas was very different from the fond memories from Donna's past. Her brother, Tom, and his wife came with their two children and aunts and uncles converged on the old home place of Donna's grandmother. Her mother was the only sibling who cared enough for the old home to buy it from the estate when Grandma Rosie died. Catherine Johnson had always loved the old home, located in downtown Greenville. She was determined that it would stay in the family as long as she had any control over it. She and Donna's father had been fortunate enough to have the financial ability to maintain the integrity of the home while updating kitchen, bathrooms and wiring. Other homes in the neighborhood were also bought by families who wanted to live in the city but enjoy a modernized home. It was a comfortable neighborhood and one that was always in demand. Houses that were put on the market sold quickly most of the time for more than the asking price.

Donna found herself looking forward to being engulfed in tradition for a few days with her mother constantly hovering over her. The shock of finding her father far more feeble than in her last visit caused Donna to reflect over her childhood. Dad had been a good father. He was interested in his children but gave them room to explore and make their own mistakes. She was lost in thought early one morning before anyone else was up. Catherine came into the kitchen to find Donna holding a cup of coffee and staring into space.

"Good morning. Where are you this morning?" Catherine chided.

"Oh, good morning Mom. You know it doesn't seem possible that Dad could be so old and feeble. It seems like yesterday that he was playing golf, maintaining the lawn and involved in several community projects. Where has all that time gone?"

"It happens before you know it. That's why I've always told you to live for today. Yesterday is over with and tomorrow hasn't come yet. You can't control either one of those days. But you can control today and what you do with it. I hope you've realized that, since you moved away. The loss of your beautiful baby can't stop you from living your life. If God is willing, you can have another child. You will always mourn your first born, but you can still love another baby. I know you. You have a lot of love to give."

"I know. I'm almost there. It's just been so hard. I have been back in church. Though I'm beginning to get disillusioned with folks who seem to only want to gossip about other church members. I'm going to look for another church."

"Well, that is one answer. But you know, folks are just human. We all have faults and we all sin. It's a good thing God can overlook all our sins. Those sins may seem unforgivable to you, but not to God. He didn't create us to be perfect. He wanted us to have choices in life. Some of those choices are good and some are bad. But with Grace he forgives them all."

"You make everything so clear. I really have missed you. I was so scared about seeing Tom, Amy and the children. I was afraid that I would resent them. Now, I don't think I will. I think I can love them like an aunt should. I can't wait for them to get here tomorrow."

Thinking back over this conversation with her mother helped Donna make the drive to First Baptist Church the Sunday after she returned home to Gainesville. It was a mammoth structure with four white columns in front, magnificent in every detail. She had talked Paul into coming with her this first time. There was something about going into a new church alone. Donna was still insecure in new settings, meeting new people. As they walked up the steps arm-in-arm Donna smiled pleasantly to the men and women they passed.

Two long carpeted aisles separated the three rows of pews. The gold carpet flowed toward the front toward the alter, over the steps to the podium and stopped at the rich walnut-stained choir loft. The choir discretely had their clothes covered with white gowns trimmed in gold. Donna and Paul were seated near the center of the church in the middle section of pews. Donna noticed all the looks they were getting. She always felt uncomfortable walking in front of other women, imagining them mentally criticizing her dress, hairstyle, or the few extra pounds she carried in the right places. Men never bothered her. She knew she got looks from them, but she also knew that they were approving looks. She had been flirted with enough in her life to know that men were attracted to her fair complexion, blonde hair and curvaceous figure. It was the women's catty remarks and aloofness that terrified Donna and made her appear just as aloof.

To get her mind off the women, Donna looked up toward the covered Baptismal and on further to the ceiling. The high walls were bordered by deeply carved moldings stained in the same walnut stain as the choir loft and the backs of the pews. Donna realized that the seats were heavily padded and covered in the same gold material as the curtain of the Baptismal.

One chandelier hung from the center of the ceiling though this was not where the majority of the light came. There were fluorescent lights cleverly hidden behind the balcony stubs and under the carved molding. But the chandelier drew her eyes and held them. She had never seen anything so beautiful in all her life. There must have been 5000 tiny bulbs hung within the structure. It was made of tier after tier of crystal and walnut shaped candles. If it were let down to the floor, it would have taken up most of the center aisle.

Finally when the Doxology began Donna looked toward the front again and for the first time she noticed the gold cross mounted to the left of the Baptismal on a walnut frame. To the right was a picture of Jesus. The familiar profile. The one she loved so. The one that made her feel that He was indeed here right at this moment. The announcements were made and Donna did not hear a single word. She was brought out of her reverie only when the choir began to sing Holy, Holy, Holy, Lord, God, Almighty. She joined in, filling her lungs and heart with the song. It was her favorite song. Maybe this was a sign. She hadn't felt this peaceful in a long time.

When she moved to Gainesville, she looked for an out-of-the-way church where she would not be expected to participate in the women's activities. She was running away from her past and not thinking about how to worship. And then she met Jenny. From that moment she was going to church to see Jenny. These were the wrong reasons to go to church. Now she could move past that experience and be part of a church, giving her whole heart to the experience of worship. She had made the right decision to come to this church. It felt like home already. She squeezed Paul's arm and he looked at her and smiled. They sat back and relaxed in the familiar atmosphere.

## Chapter 22

Jenny sat in her room alone. Drab was all she could think. Since Fred wasn't sharing the room anymore, Grandpa had bought special things for it--frilly curtains, a bedspread, a small pink fluffy rug. This was Jenny's favorite. She put it right next to her bed, so that she stepped on it first thing every morning. She would sit on the edge of her bed and slowly rub her feet on the soft ticklish fur.

This room could never be like the room Donna had made for her, but in a way it was better, because Grandpa had bought the things for her. He was family. And even though Donna and Paul seemed to want her to stay with them, they were not family.

Grandpa had told Jenny how important it was for families to stay together, especially when one of them was in trouble. She wasn't sure exactly what she could do, but she was glad he made her feel like an important part of the family.

Mr. Kittenridge was pacing the living room floor analyzing the components of his defense for Fred. Every time he had a thought that he wanted to check on for the case, he would make a quick turn toward the table to write it down and would bang his head on the hanging naked light bulb. He was generally in a foul mood today, but if Jenny came around, he would smile and pat her on the head, or sit down for a few minutes with her in his lap. She had won a special place in his heart from the first moment he saw her. She brought back memories of the way Nelda had been when she was a child.

He was building his whole case on the strong family ties and planned to show that Fred's concern for his impoverished family had made him rob the station. But it was not going to be easy. He was trying to picture his daughter as a hard-working woman, which in fact she was. But he was astonished when he saw her again after 20 years. There was no cause for her to let herself go the way she had. She could at least fix her hair and try to do some decorating in the house.

Her mousy brown hair was splashed with gray. She wore it straight, parted in the middle with the sides pushed behind her ears. It was obvious that she seldom washed it and never put a curler in it. Her loose cotton dresses hung knee-length. Any previous beauty she had was hidden somewhere deep within.

He wondered how he could make a jury believe that Nelda and Hubert truly cared about their children and were doing their best to provide and care for them.

His main problem now was finding someone to help him. The insurmountable amount of paperwork required to try a case these days took more time than the trial would. He needed to find someone who would work for minimum wage to type the Orders and Pleadings to be filed with the Court and to keep him organized. He was having difficulty finding research and files that he had created that same day. He was accustomed to having a secretary to take care of these details.

Since he didn't know anyone in town, and Nelda was in no position to know of anyone, he was at a complete loss.

He was sitting on the sofa contemplating his problem when Jenny came into the room.

"Grandpa."

"What?"

"You know, I miss Aunt Donna a lot. I know I'm not supposed to see her, but do you think I could call her and talk for a minute?"

He looked at her cautiously, but her sweet smile was more than he could resist. "Well, I suppose that would be okay. Let's see if we can find her home number."

"I know it already. I remember it from when I lived with her. Can I call her now?"

"Okay. Okay. I'll take you to the country store. I need a cigar anyway."

Jenny nervously dialed the phone, afraid that Donna wouldn't be home. From the moment Donna answered the phone Jenny could tell that Donna was glad to hear from her, but it sounded like Donna was crying. She only talked for a minute. After asking about Paul, she asked, "Is my room still the same?"

"I wouldn't change it for anything." Donna whispered. There was nothing left to say and as she started to hang up Donna said, "Now, Jenny, you tell your grandfather to call me if I can help in any way. Okay?"

"Okay, Aunt Donna, I will." She hung up the phone. Grandpa bought her a pack of chewing gum, but she forgot to give him Donna's message.

That evening as Mr. Kittenridge was helping Nelda set the table Jenny overheard him talking about the amount of work he had to do and that he could use some help. Then she remembered what Donna had said.

"Grandpa, Grandpa. Aunt Donna said she would be glad to help any way she could. Call her, okay? Call her. She'll help you. She's very smart. I know she can do something to help."

# Chapter 23

Donna had not been sleeping well lately. The night before she was supposed to start work for Mr. Kittenridge, she took a sleeping pill so she would get a good night's sleep and have her wits about her.

Consequently she overslept and was in a panic when she finally woke up at 7:00 a.m. She rushed to the kitchen to make coffee add start the bacon. She returned to the bedroom to wake Paul.

He pulled her down to kiss her and didn't want to let her get up. Mornings were his favorite times for love-making, but today there was no time. She wrestled free.

"Come on Paul. You'll be late."

"So?"

"Well, then, I'll be late."

"So?"

"I need to be on time. It's very important to Fred and Jenny."

"I thought you had given up on her."

"I have. I mean, I know she can never be mine. But I must help her family, if I can."

"And tough luck 'ole Paul."

"No, Paul. Really Let's hurry. Okay? I promise to give you quality time tonight."

She left the room and Paul turned over and sighed as he threw the covers back. He shook his head at his confusion over the path his wife had taken. Her moods here lately had just about stretched his patience. She was, at once, sullen, moody and introspective. And then a miraculous change overcame her, and she was energetic, upbeat and anxious to get on with their lives. He liked this Donna best. But he wasn't sure the other one wouldn't return at a moment's notice. In fact, he knew she would return if there were any rejection from the little girl who had stolen her heart.

Donna paced the kitchen floor, first looking at the eggs frying on the stove and then looking out the window at the low clouds hanging over the house as if they would protect her from the unknown outside world. She felt warmth in the clouds. She understood Nature. The impending storm was predictable and comforting. It reminded her that God was still in control of the universe. She leaned into the window with both hands gripping the edge of the sink. She peered into the depths of the clouds and whispered a plea to God to guide her through the day. It was the most she could invest in her belief for now. If God was up there somewhere and heard her prayer and helped her through this day, then she could open up to Him a little more. But until she had confidence that He was listening and that He cared, she couldn't trust in Him completely. Not just yet.

Paul appeared in the doorway, smiling. She heard his footsteps and turned to hand him his plate of eggs, bacon and toast. As she saw his tall, strong frame, she caught her breath. It still amazed her that after all these years he could elicit that reaction from her. He was more dear to her today, than on their wedding day. She smiled at him, as she handed him his breakfast. "My knight in shining armor."

"Princess," he acknowledged as he brushed her cheek with a kiss. "What's your agenda for the day?"

"Don't know yet. At this point, I'm available for whatever Mr. Kittenridge needs."

"Will you be late tonight?"

"Oh, I doubt it. But, just in case, I'll leave you a message on the answering machine if I see I'll be late." For the first time Donna wished that she had invested in a cell phone as Paul had encouraged her to do over the years.

"Try hard to be here when I get home. You know I hate coming home when you're not here."

The day was a flurry of phone calls, setting appointments and typing some documents. Mr. Kittenridge was an able trial lawyer and had a game plan in mind. Her support was going to allow him to move forward with the defense more quickly. He asked if she could accompany him to some of the interviews, so that she could take notes.

It was six o'clock before she realized it. They had moved their work to a table in the county library and she used a typewriter available to library patrons. They both realized that this would not work for long. They needed the privacy of an office and the availability of a computer. She was making calls to local real estate companies to see if they had an office for rent for a few months without a long-term lease. When she saw that she had broken her promise to Paul, she quickly stacked her notes and headed for the door. "Mr. Kittenridge, I'll see you tomorrow. I must get home to my husband, now. Where shall we meet tomorrow?"

Luckily the library was in town. The drive home only took a few minutes. When she arrived, Paul's car was in the garage. As she entered the back door she smelled the wonderful aroma of stir-fried chicken and rice. Paul was wearing a frilly apron and pointing toward a candlelit table and singing as he greeted her.

That night as Donna lay down to sleep, she closed her eyes and thanked God for the day, for her supportive husband and for the love of a grandfather who would rearrange his life to protect his grandson. She asked for God to bless the Moore family and protect Jenny in that family. As she prayed these prayers, she felt a comfort wrap around her that she hadn't felt in many years. She asked God to stay with her for the night. For the first time in a long, long time she was praying for someone other than herself. She had no desire in her heart to manipulate Jenny or to encourage Jenny to return to her house. Her only desire was for the well-being of the Moores.

She fell asleep immediately into a deep, soul-refreshing sleep. There was no tossing and turning tonight.

# Chapter 24

Jenny walked out to the small coop of breeders. The larger layer houses took up most of the yard and all of their time. But this was her favorite spot.

She would stand there and watch the rooster jump on the unsuspecting hen's back and peck her head and neck until she submitted to him even though she did not do it willingly.

This gave Jenny some pleasure that she could not understand. It seemed to be the natural way. Not like back there in the house. Her father submitting to her mother. Her brother submitting to her mother. She knew if she ever got away from here she would be the one to bear the marks on her neck and head, and she was reassured by this knowledge.

She was standing there when she heard a car in the driveway. She turned and looked down the driveway as

Donna stepped out of her car. Seeing Donna always made her happy. She threw up her hand at Donna and began running toward her, forgetting immediately the hens and her thoughts about nature's cruelty surrounding their life cycle.

Donna watched as Jenny ran down the driveway. Jenny's smile was innocent and compelling. She loved Donna, but not as a mother. She was intrigued, impressed and inquisitive about Donna's life. Donna exposed her to a lifestyle that Jenny had never imagined. She wanted to be a part of the things Donna had shown her. She wanted to see and do more. But down deep inside, she still hungered for the love and acceptance of her own mother.

Donna looked at Jenny in a different way today, too. She saw a bright, innocent, happy child that made her miss her own daughter—ache for a child of her own. But gone was the desperation to claim Jenny. She realized that Jenny belongs with her family.

It had come to her last night as she lay in bed thinking about her life with Paul and Jenny's life with her family. She had an overwhelming release from her selfish hopes. She only wanted what was best for Jenny. Now she even felt connected to the whole Moore family. She realized that God had released her. She had not known she was praying. She had relied on God all her life for so many decisions. Why had she been avoiding Him now? There was no way to be happy thinking only of her own wants and desires.

The Moores had more problems than any family should have to face. Donna had decided that she could make a difference in their lives. She would make that her goal from this moment on.

Donna stooped to accept Jenny's outstretched arms and receive a big hug. "What's up?" she asked.

Jenny's response was typical of a child. "I'm bored. Everybody's busy and not paying attention to me. My Ma hasn't even yelled at me today. I wish we could go to the lake house."

Donna stood and took Jenny's hand. "Now, you know that's a good idea. After all this business with Fred is over, we'll take your whole family there for a day of fishing and picnicking."

"You will? Oh, that would be so much fun. I've never been anywhere for fun with Ma and Pa. Do you think they'd go?"

"I promise you they will go. Let's go see what's going on inside your house."

"Oh, Grandpa and Ma and Pa are just sittin' at the kitchen table talkin'."

When Donna and Jenny reached the kitchen door, she overheard Nelda and Hubert discussing their financial situation. They had always been poor, but this situation with Fred had drained any money they had put aside. Court costs and the loss of Hubert's income from the chickens had them wondering how they would buy groceries and pay utilities. Just as she knocked she heard Nelda tell Hubert that she had to go to work to help pay the court costs.

Hubert was adamant that his wife would not work outside of the home. "I've always looked after this family and I intend to keep on looking after it. Anyway, you ain't got no skills. Where'd you work?"

"I don't know, but I know I could do something. I was a pretty good student."

Donna's knock prevented Hubert's response.

Nelda approached the door hesitantly. Donna asked if she could come in. Nelda opened the door and motioned for Donna to go into the living room. Mr. Kittenridge looked up with a smile as Jenny and Donna entered the room. The initial smile was for his granddaughter. "Oh, Donna. I'm working on some research today. I don't know right this minute what you could do for me. I'm so sorry you drove all this way for nothing. I really need to break down and get a cell phone. I've put it off all these years. It just seemed so confining. But I really need one here, since Nelda and Hubert don't have a phone."

Donna smiled, "Me too. Maybe my drive wasn't wasted. I overheard Mr. and Mrs. Moore discussing their financial situation. She is interested in finding a job. I think I might be able to help her get prepared for her job search."

"Oh, that would be a wonderful idea. I know that Nelda would feel so much better about herself if she would just fix up a little. If she got out and met other people maybe she would regain some of that gracefulness I remember in her."

"Maybe you could just mention to her that I would be willing to assist her," Donna said.

"Yes, yes. I'll go talk to her right now. Just sit down right here. I'll be back."

At first Nelda didn't want to take any help from Donna. In some respect she admired Donna for her self-assuredness, her poise and her beauty. But she had a deep fear that Donna would become the mother to Jenny that she could never be. She had made the choice to push Jenny away, but seeing her respond to Donna as she had made Nelda yearn for that close relationship some mothers and daughters had. But for the present time, Fred had to be the focus of the entire family. She needed a job to help pay the bills. If Donna could help her, then she needed to swallow her pride and accept the help.

Donna had begun stopping for breakfast at a little café that had been opened in the early 1940's. It was located on the square across from the courthouse. It seemed to be the place where all the local businessmen started their day. She enjoyed sitting quietly, listening to the conversations around her as she sipped her coffee and watched them eat a standard breakfast of eggs, bacon and toast. She listened to the hype about eating too much fat, but her cholesterol had always been low, her LDL levels were always high and her HDL levels were low. She exercised regularly and had no family history of heart problems. She found it difficult to feel guilty about this recent ritual. She got her energy and vitality from breakfast.

On this particular morning, she overheard the counter waitress and the cook talking about the need for another person to help in the mornings. They planned to place a sign in the window that morning. Breakfast was their main meal. They closed at 2 p.m., offering only sandwiches and hot dogs and hamburgers for lunch. The hours seemed perfect for

Nelda. Donna perked up as she left the café. She couldn't wait to tell Nelda about the job opening.

Donna had spent the previous week taking Nelda to the beauty parlor, department store for a few simple coordinating skirts, pants and blouses. A quick trip to the drug store supplied Nelda with the makeup basics. Donna still could not get over the difference in Nelda with these few changes. Even Jenny was impressed.

"Wow, Ma. What did you do?" was her response when Donna escorted Nelda home the day her hair had been cut and styled in a short-cropped look that was perfect for Nelda's slender face. A little highlighting detracted from the graying and gave her hair body. She looked 10 years younger.

Donna practically ran from the car to the front door of the Moore's house. Nelda came to the door in a pair of khaki slacks with a chamois shirt. Donna smiled, "I have some great news. The café across from the courthouse has an opening for help. They just put the sign in the widow. If we go now, you could be the first person to apply. Can you get away now?"

Nelda froze. This is what she wanted, but she suddenly became terribly frightened. She had been such a recluse in the past few years that she wasn't sure she could face the real world. Donna understood her hesitancy. "I'll come with you Nelda. This will be a perfect starting place for you. They close at 2 p.m. You'll have the entire afternoon to take care of things around here."

Nelda slowly opened the door for Donna to enter and quickly turned to walk into the room, but not before Donna saw her trembling hands. Instinctively, Donna patted her gently on the shoulder and said, "Let's tell Hubert. I think you have a good chance at this job if we hurry."

Nelda realized how much she has missed in life by not keeping herself up. She was terrified of interviewing for a job. She didn't know how to talk to strangers anymore. She wanted to lock herself up in her bedroom and pretend there was no job at the café. But she meekly led Donna to the kitchen table where Hubert was sorting through a stack of bills. "Hubert, Mrs. Whitsfield saw a help wanted sign in the café downtown. She thinks I might be able to get that job. She's gonna take me there now to talk with the owner before someone else applies."

Hubert looked up at her and then glared at Donna. "What do you mean? There is a job for you right here. I'll take care of my family. You don't need to go out looking for a public job."

"We could use the money, Hubert. You've just been sittin' here tryin to figure out how to pay the bills. Maybe I can help you get the money to pay those bills."

"That's not your place!" he shouted as he threw the bills on the table.

"Get mad if you want. I'm goin' with Donna," she said with more authority and determination than she felt.

Donna smiled. "Way to go Nelda," she thought.

When they reached the café, Donna was nervous for Nelda. It was like having a child apply for her first job. She sat in the car, straining her neck to see inside. It seemed forever before Nelda emerged with a huge smile on her face. "I start in the morning," she said as she opened the door.

The following days were a whirlwind for the Moore family. There was an energy and excitement that had never been a part of their low-key humble way of life. Nelda was leaving the house by 4:30 a.m. to get to the restaurant. That left Jenny and Hubert alone to take care of breakfast and set the routine for the day. Jenny wanted to be a part of helping Fred. Nelda had told her that the reason she must go to work was to help get Fred out of jail. Jenny was eager to be helpful. Hubert tried cooking eggs for breakfast while Jenny set the table. They were an odd pair. They had never been alone for any extended period of time and didn't have the warm father-daughter relationship that would have made the mornings an easy time. But as the days went by they began talking as they completed their tasks. Jenny learned that her father had a sense of humor. He began to smile more. Her grandfather even began dropping by unexpectedly to spend some time with them. He had moved to a motel a few days after his arrival. There simply wasn't enough room in the house for him. He and Hubert awkwardly began talking. It seemed that Mr. Kittenridge couldn't find out enough about Hubert. He seemed genuinely interested in what Hubert had to say.

He learned that Hubert had had big dreams for his chicken farm. He was encouraged to find out that Hubert wasn't happy eking out the living they had had. Hubert and Nelda had even been successful the first few years of their marriage. They had saved money to improve the chicken houses and expand the business. They had bought the adjacent land for that expansion. There was a dilapidated church on the property but it had been abandoned for years. Hubert planned to bulldoze it and build the new houses on that land. But before he could arrange for the bulldozing, a seminar graduate showed up at his door one morning asking about the church. He too had a dream. There was no other church in this part of the county in those days, and he wanted to restore and revitalize the church. He had a vision of the community worshipping in the abandoned building again. He felt that God had told him that this was his destiny.

Hubert listened intently. He knew about dreams. He believed that God had a plan for each person. He felt that this young man was led by God and was doing His will. He agreed to deed a portion of the property to the church for worship, but warned the young minister that he was going to build additional chicken houses on the back part of the property, because that was his life's work.

The minister was dynamic. He drew crowds of worshippers. In a period of months, the old church was restored and overflowed each Sunday. Hubert was continuing to save his money for the additional four chicken houses.

The day Hubert received his building permit to begin construction he proudly posted the notice on a tree at the side of the road. That evening he was visited by the young minister, who had already received several calls from his congregation who were upset and alarmed about the notice. The minister had gone to the courthouse and gotten copies of an ordinance that prohibited building or expanding a business within 200 yards of a church. Hubert's chicken houses would be 150 yards behind the church. The minister warned, demanded and finally, threatened Hubert to honor the ordinance.

Hubert was dumbfounded. He reminded the minister that he had told him he was going to build the chicken houses when he deeded the property to the church. But that did not matter any longer. The church was successful and profitable. The minister didn't want to lose his congregation.

Hubert went to a lawyer. There was no hope. He spent all his savings for the chicken houses on the lawyer's fee. Even if he won the case, he wouldn't have the money to build the houses. He was devastated. He gave up. He dropped the case and he dropped the church. He said he would never set his foot in a church again. He had kept his word.

Nelda agreed. They lived literally within the "arms of the church" but their lives were outside the church family. Eventually, after Jenny was born, Nelda changed her mind about attending church. She felt that Jenny could benefit from association with church members. She did not care about the sermons.

There was a different preacher now. The young minister only stayed a few years and then he left the small country church for a bigger, more profitable church in Atlanta. His sermons were seen on TV now, but not by Nelda or Hubert. They never spoke his name, never talked about what had transpired so many years ago, but they both lost some of their souls in that encounter with the young "man of God".

On hearing this information, Mr. Kittenridge felt so helpless. If only he had known about their problems, he could have helped in some way. At least he could have been supportive and visited them. They could have visited with him. He could have been a part of Fred's life. And maybe, just maybe, all this wouldn't be happening to Fred. His guilt tore at him. But he wanted to hear more.

He wanted to examine the deed to the church. He wanted to understand how Hubert's good intentions had gone wrong. He went immediately to the courthouse to the deed room and completed a title search of Hubert's property and the church's property. He needed to trace the events and build a timeline.

## Chapter 25

Nelda's life had changed dramatically since she took the job at the café. She arose early each morning. By the time she returned home at 2:30 p.m., she was exhausted, but she couldn't sit down. There was so much to be done.

It seemed she and Hubert had no time to talk anymore. He was always out in the chicken houses and after dinner they were both so tired that they fell into bed with very little conversation. Nelda was beginning to appreciate having her father around. It had been a long time, but she remembered how safe and comfortable she always felt as a little girl. She thought her father could protect her and would always be there for her. She remembered him kissing scratches and scrapes and holding her hand as he walked with her in the evenings. Sometimes they would sit quietly on the porch listening to the chirp of the crickets and the squeak of the swing as his foot pushed them gently until she fell asleep nuzzled next to his warm side.

The teenage years had been tough for them. She wanted to be independent. He wanted to protect her. It ended so terribly. Neither one got what they sought.

The years of hardship Nelda and Hubert had experienced built a bond between them. Their marriage was solid and she had no intention of letting her father come between them now. Even if the passion had ended years before, they were united in the commitment to the marriage. They had taken vows. Marriage was forever—until death.

As she placed dirty dishes in the sink she heard the car in the driveway. She knew instinctively it was her father. He sometimes would come over after dinner. Never wanting to cause a hardship by eating with them. She thought he must be lonely. Some nights he would talk about the trial. But most nights he would sit quietly without saying much. Jenny would keep him occupied until her bedtime and then he would try to make conversation with Nelda. After a few ill-fated tries he would excuse himself and return to the motel until morning.

She knew he came by the house after she left for work. She was glad that he was building a relationship with his granddaughter.

Tonight he opened the door without knocking and almost bounded into the room. His face was beaming. She couldn't imagine why he was so happy.

"Nelda! I have some wonderful news for you and Hubert. Where is he?"

"He's making his nightly rounds of the houses to be sure the chickens haven't turned over their water and food. Why?"

"The deed...it isn't worth the paper it's written on."

"What deed?"

"The deed to the church for their expansion. There was no consideration, no money paid for it. Therefore there was no legal sale. The land still belongs to you and Hubert."

"What do we want with the land the church is on? We can't do nothing with it."

"Anything."

"What?"

"You can't do anything with it."

"That's what I said."

"No. You said nothing. Oh, never mind. Nelda I can't believe you don't understand. You were so bright as a young girl. What happened? Why did you give up?" This was the first time he had ever spoken to her in this way. She was immediately defensive.

"Some things ain't...aren't...that important. When you don't have food on the table, or you can't pay your electric bill, who cares how you talk. Everyone up here talks this way."

"No they don't. Some lazy folks do. But not you Nelly." This was the first time he had called her that in so many years that Nelda had forgotten his pet name for her. Tears immediately filled her eyes.

When he saw her tears he reached for her hand. "My Nelly. I wanted so much for you growing up. I just wanted the wrong things. I'm sorry. You and Hubert have had more trouble than any one couple should have to endure in one lifetime. I'm going to help you Nelly. I'm going to free Fred. And I'm going to get you some money from the church for the land they built on."

"No, you're not." Hubert walked into the room and heard the last part of the sentence. "I gave that land to the church. It's theirs to use how they want."

"But Hubert, it's not legal. They didn't give you money for it. Even one dollar. There must be consideration, at least a dollar for a sale to take place."

"I don't care about the money. I don't go back on my word. Some folks do. Some folks that I reckon should always keep their word, don't'. So, I'm going to."

"But Hubert, you and Nelly need the money."

"Nelly?"

"Nelda. You could sell this place. And with that money and what you'd get for this farm you could build somewhere else."

"I don't want no where else. This is our home. I'm going to support my family and take care of them."

Mr. Kittenridge realized that there was no sense in arguing any more tonight. It was getting late and Hubert had his mind made up. He would just have to find another way to convince him.

## Chapter 26

Nelda watched Hubert from the kitchen window. She was getting dressed for work when she heard him get up and go outside. She always made enough coffee for him when she made her breakfast. He had a cup in his hand now as he stood in the glow of the spotlight hanging on the edge of the house. He was looking toward the land that the church was on. He was not moving. But she knew what he was thinking. He wondered if he had done the right thing years ago deeding the land to the church.

She supported his decision then and she wouldn't back away from that now. He was a good man with a good heart. He had no way of knowing that his decision would turn out the way it had and hurt his family. Even though his decision didn't work out for them, he wouldn't go back on his word, no matter what her father found out. She knew that.

While Nelda was working that morning Donna came in for breakfast. She did that sometimes. Nelda had begun looking forward to her visits. Donna was everything she always thought she would be. She wasn't jealous of Donna. She was just intrigued by her.

Apparently her father had already talked to Donna about the deed to the property. Donna was anxious to talk with Nelda about it. But Nelda was busy and in no mood to justify their actions.

To her surprise Donna seemed to understand and didn't push the issue. She visited for a while and asked if she could come over to see Jenny later in the day. Nelda agreed. Donna wanted Jenny to continue her piano lessons. Nelda had made her stop the lessons when the situation with Fred became public. But she didn't want to talk with Nelda about it here or now.

When Donna arrived at the Moore house that afternoon, she had her plan clearly laid out. There was no rush to discuss the deed. First Donna wanted to establish a routine with Jenny again. Jenny could use the distraction and she really had a talent for the piano. At first Donna made small talk with Jenny. Then she casually asked her if she missed practicing the piano. At first Jenny looked sad, "Yes. I miss it a lot. But Ma says it would hurt Fred if I keep taking the lessons. So it's okay."

Donna was amazed at the innocence of that simple statement. It was apparent that there was no issue. If it hurt Fred, then Jenny wouldn't do it. Donna realized that Nelda and Hubert had given their children much more than material gifts. They had supplied them with values that would carry them the rest of their lives. It was hard for her to believe that at one time she thought that Jenny was being abused by her Mother. It was clear that both Nelda and Hubert loved their children. Donna hoped that she would always remember that things weren't always as they seemed. She wasn't sure what happened to Fred to make him take part in the theft.

"What if I make it alright? What if I make sure that it won't hurt Fred for you to go over to the church to take your piano lessons and practice? Would you do it then?"

"Yes, yes, yes! But how would you do that?"

"Let me worry about that. I see your Mom coming up the drive now. Let me talk with her."

"Okay," Jenny trailed the words after her as she ran to meet Nelda walking up the drive.

Donna took a deep breath. She knew she had a hard sell ahead of her.

## Chapter 27

At first Nelda had been adamant. She didn't want Jenny anywhere around the church. But Donna prevailed upon her love for Jenny and the value that Jenny would get from piano lessons.

Rev. McClure joyfully welcomed Jenny back to the church, even though it was only for piano lessons, not preaching. He knew that there were a lot of ways to minister to people, especially children. Donna now had a full schedule. She worked with Mr. Kittenridge each morning running errands and typing legal papers. But one afternoon each week, she left her chores and drove to the Moore house. She knew Jenny would be more comfortable if she went to the lessons with Donna. The first day back at the piano she played as if she had been practicing every day. Donna knew it was the right decision for Jenny. It could change her life.

On the afternoons that Jenny was at her lessons, Nelda and Hubert were alone at the farm. She came home from work by 2:30 p.m., just as Jenny was leaving for the church. At first, these afternoons became the times when Nelda and Hubert would sit at the kitchen table and talk. Nelda couldn't remember how long it had been since they were comfortable talking to each other. Gradually, Hubert felt comfortable reaching for her hand as they talked. Their dreams had been shattered many years ago. But the ordeal with Fred seemed to cement their future. How could they ever recover from the shame they felt for what Fred did? And how could he ever lead a normal life when he did get out of jail?

Nelda yielded to Hubert's touch. She needed him now, too. His large, rough hands brought such comfort to her. She wanted to remain in their safety forever. As the weeks passed, Nelda began to look forward to the afternoons when she and Hubert were alone. She longed for the intimacy they had shared in their youth. Hubert longed for that too...and more.

They began to take short walks over the farm, making plans and dreaming as if everything would work out for them.

On one of their walks, Hubert boldly put his arm around Nelda. She leaned into him. His heart began to beat rapidly. He looked down at her. She met his gaze. Their kiss was as innocent as a first kiss, but gradually both of their needs took over. They returned to the house for an afternoon of lovemaking that shocked and satisfied them both like new lovers. From that day on, Jenny's piano lessons became the intimate time for Nelda and Hubert.

Nelda's job restored her confidence in making suggestions regarding the farm. Her renewed interest in the farm made Hubert excited about her return from work each day. He found himself looking down the driveway several times each afternoon, full of ideas and suggestions he wanted to discuss with her. He looked forward to watching her walk toward the house. The spring in her step convinced him that she was happy in spite of all their troubles. She beamed when she saw him coming around the corner of the house. His dirty arms and sweaty shirt represented his hard work for her and the children.

She loved his determination and tenacity. Her beauty began to shine through the years showing on her face. To Hubert, she was more beautiful than when they married.

While Nelda and Hubert were rebuilding their marriage, Donna was rebuilding her relationship with Jenny. She was also delving into the history of the church. She felt that somehow this knowledge would help Mr. Kittenridge. She wasn't sure how, but she felt a need to do something.

Then Donna remembered those first conversations with Mrs. Milligan. Mrs. Milligan had shared bits and pieces of church history with her over the months. Donna decided that she would start with Mrs. Milligan. She wasn't sure how her interest in the church's history would be perceived, but she counted on her perception that Mrs. Milligan had rather gossip than question Donna's motives.

The phone call went more smoothly than Donna could have hoped. Mrs. Milligan, Kate as she asked Donna to call her, invited Donna over for tea. Kate was intrigued with Donna. Their first encounter had ended so abruptly with Donna walking out on their meeting. She knew that Donna wanted something from her now, or she wouldn't have called. The question was "what did Donna want?"

It had been a long time since Donna shared afternoon tea with anyone. The last time had been in Atlanta when she and her Service League friends met to discuss committee work. Even after she and Paul had moved to Gainesville, she still enjoyed a break around 4 o'clock with a cup of honey-flavored tea, putting her feet up and relaxing on the back porch for 15 or 20 minutes. It seemed to be the turning point in her day, when she forgot goals and tasks and began anticipating the evening with Paul.

Kate Milligan was all smiles as she opened the door to her two-story colonial home on Green Street, one of the few left as private homes. Donna caught her breath as she stepped into the large foyer with mirror-like hardwood floors. The mahogany stair railing swept to the right and then to the left as it wrapped itself toward the second story balcony. Donna's interior design background made her want to explore every inch of this lovely old home, but she was here on a mission and there was no time for fantasy.

"Come in Mrs. Whitsfield. I'm delighted that you called me. This way into the sitting room."

Donna tried not to gape as she seated herself across from Kate. She accepted her cup of tea and waved off cream and sugar. "I do have a reason for meeting with you." She thought it was best to be forthright. "You know I've been involved with the Moore family and their situation with Fred's trial. I'm trying to discover the history of their situation so that I might be able to help them."

"Well, I thought it had something to do with them. Rumor has it that you have taken the child, Jenny, to live with you. That's why she hasn't been around the church lately."

Donna's face turned crimson with the guilt she felt, "No, Jenny is not living with me. I'm trying to figure out a way to help the family financially. There seems to be some confusion about their land and the land the church is located on. Do you know anything about that?"

"All I know is that we can't expand the church because of their dilapidated house and the chicken farm."

"How long have you attended the church?"

"Oh, about five years. But the membership has grown so much in those five years. We need to expand for classrooms and parking. How are we going to continue to grow with the boundaries the Moores have set around us?"

"Did anyone at the church ever think about those things before they began the expansion program? This is the Moore's home. They have lived there for over 20 years. It is their land." Donna was trying not to get emotional, but it was so difficult to see the contrast in what Kate Milligan had materially and what little the Moores had. And Mrs. Milligan wanted to take the little that they had away from them.

"Well, we offered to buy their farm. I think we offered them a fair price."

"Was it enough for them to build a new home and new chicken houses?"

"Well, I don't know. How much could those old houses cost anyway?"

"The problem, Mrs. Milligan, Kate, is that if they were to start over, they would need to build new chicken houses which can cost over $100,000 each. They must ventilate them and supply automatic feeders and watering to prevent spills and disease. As long as they keep their current houses, the suppliers will give chickens to them. If they move, they will have to meet the new standards in order to get chickens." Donna was proud that she had remembered so much from her reading on chicken farming.

"Well, no. I didn't know that. We don't want to put them on the street, but what are we to do?"

Donna felt a weakening in Kate's reserve, so she took a chance on that sliver of softness and shared what Mr. Kittenridge had told her. "About 12 years go the Moores had a successful chicken farm with enough land to expand as profits permitted. At that time, the church as you know it was a dilapidated building with no preacher and no members. A young minister came to town and when he saw the church building, he felt that God had led him to that spot to bring worship services into the county. He talked with Hubert Moore about his dreams. Hubert and Nelda agreed to give the land where the dilapidated church sat to the future church. Over the next year they supplied the money for restoration and supplies. The young minister became full of himself and wanted to expand the church. He wanted more land from the Moore's farm. The initial land transaction was very specific about the land restriction that would apply to the church because the Moores planned to expand their chicken business. But the young preacher found an old statute that said that Mr. Moore could not expand his chicken farm any closer to the church. By this time the chicken business had bottomed out and the Moores had very little left each month to live on. They could not fight the church's expansion, but they refused to leave their home and their dreams. In time, the young minister moved on to a bigger church in Atlanta and Rev. McClure was called as the minister. The interesting thing is that the deed was never executed properly. The church grounds still legally belong to the Moores. They don't want the church property, but they also don't want to be harassed by church members. Isn't it the Christian spirit to help the Moores now when they are in need? They are the closest neighbors the church has."

Mrs. Milligan sat silently for a few minutes. She was embarrassed that she had been so outspoken about the Moores. She should have gotten all the facts before she began her campaign to move them. She silently asked God for forgiveness for being so cruel to these good people. "Okay. What do we need to do?"

"Well, first of all, they need cash to help pay court costs. And their house needs some fixing up. What do you think?"

"I think I can definitely handle that. Just give me some time. I have coordinated the largest fund-raising event in the city for the past 5 years. I certainly can manage to coordinate a little painting and repairing."

Donna was pleased that her instincts had been right. Christian people do help others in need. She left Kate with a renewed faith in church members.

The next Sunday Kate Milligan stood at the front of the church and told the members about the origin of the property deed. The church immediately decided to pull together and fix up the Moore's house. They realized that the church never paid Hubert back for the well he had dug for water for the church, or for the building materials that Hubert purchased for the church renovation. The church had no money at the time to buy supplies and there were no rich people in the church at that time.

The sermon was forgotten. By early afternoon a team was formed to renovate the Moore's house. They planned to have a crew show up the next morning and begin the work.

Hubert and Nelda were surprised when the first truck pulled into their driveway at 7 a.m. Monday morning. Nelda had the day off and they were just beginning the day's chores. Members piled out of the truck, unloading materials, paint and tools. Hubert walked toward them protesting. "What are you doing? I didn't hire anyone. What do you want?"

Just as he approached the workers, Kate Milligan's silver Mercedes abruptly stopped at his side. "Hello, Mr. Moore. You don't know me. But I'm a member of the church. We found out that we owe you for our church restoration and for supporting it when no one else would. We're here to partially repay that debt. Now, move out of the way. These men have a lot of work to do."

Hubert had no choice. The men were already spilling all over the grounds, in the house and chicken houses. Over the next few weeks, the church members hung sheet-rock, insulated, painted, rewired, installed new plumbing, carpeted, and planted grass, flowers and shrubs. Church members donated time and supplies from their businesses. The women made curtains. One member was a successful furniture dealer and gave them new furniture. Hubert didn't want to take favors, but they overwhelmed him. And they insisted that they were just repaying the loan he had made to the church so many years ago.

## Chapter 28

Jenny wasn't sure how to react to all the attention her family was getting from the church lately. That first morning when all those men came into the yard, she was a little afraid. She had never seen so many people around her house.

Her Ma had been so nervous, wringing her hands, laughing and crying at the same time. And her Pa...well, he just wasn't the same since that day. He smiled a lot now. He began helping the workers when he realized that his protests were unheeded. But they told him to take care of his chicken business and leave the refurbishing to them. He tried, but he just couldn't keep his eyes off the men and the work they were doing. Right before his eyes, his home was turning into a cozy cottage. It actually began to take the shape of the dream house Nelda had told him about so many years ago. At the end of the renovations, there was enough lumber left to build a deck off of the kitchen and around the back of the house under the dining room window. The old oak tree between the house and the first chicken house was a perfect canopy for the deck. He knew Nelda would be pleased to have a place for them to sit in the evenings after the dishes were done.

Each afternoon when Nelda returned from her job at the café, she stood in the driveway amazed at what magic had been performed in her absence. She began looking forward to going to work each day, just so she could get surprised with the progress each afternoon. At first, she was aggravated because her house was in total disarray. Even though they had very little furniture and fixings, she knew where everything was. During the renovations, she couldn't find anything. But the third week of the work, she could already see that these improvements were going to make her life so easy. One church member had donated new kitchen cabinets. He had made them for a custom house he was building, but the purchaser wanted a different style; so he donated them to the Moores. The city's oldest appliance store donated a new stove, refrigerator and a dishwasher. New flooring was installed from a church member who had remnants from other projects that just fit Nelda and Hubert's home. Some of the carpenters insisted that the floor plan needed to be expanded to include a bathroom in Nelda and Hubert's bedroom and that their bedroom should be enlarged. A French door was installed so that they could walk onto the deck from their bedroom.

Jenny also looked forward to the afternoons. She would run out to her mother and give her a tour of everything that had been done that day. She gave great details of how the men had worked and where they had put their belongings. None of them understood the scope of the project until it was finished. The building activity and excitement took the edge off the activity that Mr. Kittenridge was involved in for Fred.

When the construction started, Mr. Kittenridge began his daily visits after Nelda returned from work. That way he could share his progress and concerns with her and Hubert at the same time. He was usually invited to stay for dinner, which would result in him staying and visiting with Jenny for a while. They were becoming as close as any grandparent and grandchild. He and Nelda were even beginning to reconnect in some ways.

He decided that there was no point in pursuing the legal matter of the deed transfer from Hubert to the church. He knew Hubert well enough now to understand that Hubert would never allow him to interfere with that gift.

The family visited Fred each Wednesday afternoon as soon as Nelda got off work. Only Jenny was left out of these visits. Nelda didn't want her exposed to the inside of the jail, or the men who resided there. Hubert and Mr. Kittenridge would meet Nelda outside the café and they would walk across the square to the jail. They were only allowed to stay 30 minutes. Nelda and Hubert both felt that 30 minutes a week was far too little time to spend with their son.

## Chapter 29

Jenny approached her piano lessons with such intensity. She played as if her whole heart flowed through her fingers. Beginner's songs that normally sounded choppy and stilted with other young pianists had a beauty that brought tears to Donna's eyes. She vowed to herself that she would make sure Jenny would be allowed to continue these lessons as long as she loved the piano and wanted to continue playing.

Some nights before falling asleep Jenny would practice her songs in her mind. She would imagine the keys laid out across her covers on her chest and would finger out a melody and hear it ringing in her heart as surely as if the music was playing in the room. She never loved anything as much as the music from the piano. She would do it all day long if she could. Maybe someday she would own a piano and could play whenever she chose.

She closed her eyes and thanked God for Donna and for the piano lessons that Donna had made possible. Donna had been a special friend. She loved her differently than she loved anyone in her entire life. Not like she loved her Mother or her Father or Fred. Not even like she loved her Grandpa. In some ways it was a more special love because Donna was not family. Family should do things for each other. Donna didn't have to do any of the things she did for Jenny. Her last words were for God to look after Fred in that scary place.

She knew Fred was scared. Oh, he would try to be brave. He wouldn't let Ma or Pa know it, but Jenny saw his vulnerable side that they never saw. She knew he was lonely, like she had been before Donna. Only Fred had no one like Donna in his life. She was sad for that. Fred needed someone. Maybe if he had had someone, he wouldn't have tried to rob that store and he wouldn't be in jail.

When Jenny returned home after her piano lessons, there was a different feeling in the house. Most times

Ma would be smiling and sometimes even singing. Pa would be hanging around in the kitchen, talking to Ma and laughing when Jenny came in the door. He even stayed and helped with supper on these days. Even though piano lessons were her love, coming home afterward was beginning to be her favorite time of the week.

Today, Ma even asked her what songs she had played. Jenny thought that Nelda was still upset about the piano lessons. Maybe she changed her mind. Wouldn't that be wonderful if Ma would want her to play the piano? Maybe even come to the lessons someday. Could she ever hope that they could buy a piano and put it in the living room? It seemed that anything was possible now.

Since things were going so well, Jenny decided to ask something she had felt for a long time. "Ma, when can I go see Fred? I miss him so. He's my brother and he's been gone a long time. I want to see him!"

Nelda looked at Hubert, "Jenny, we just don't think it's a good idea. The jail is a horrible place for a little girl."

"I don't care! It's a horrible place for Fred too. I want to see him. I need to tell him that I love him and want him to come home."

Hubert shrugged his shoulders. Anything seemed possible these days. "Let us see what we can do, Jen. We'll talk with your Grandpa and see if he can help. Okay?"

That seemed to pacify her for tonight. Dinner smelled wonderful. The short winter days made the workers go home early, but there was plenty to do to fill the evening hours. Grandpa would come over and they would sit and talk for hours. Jenny would listen for a while and then she would drop off to sleep in Grandpa's lap or on the floor at his feet. Ma used to make her go to bed early, but since Fred's trouble, she let her stay up as long as she stayed awake. Then Pa would carry her to her bed where Ma would put on her pajamas and tuck her in. These were the good times. It wasn't quite fair that they were good times for her and such bad times for Fred.

## Chapter 30

      Fred was getting so thin. His eyes were sunken behind dark circles, which gave him a crazed look. He was afraid most of the time, but would not let anyone see him cry. He only cried softly after the lights went out each night. He knew that if the other prisoners heard him, they would taunt him…or worse. He heard cries from other cells late in the night. These were cries of pain, not simply the loneliness Fred felt. He knew terrible things happened to some of the young boys when they had to share cells.

      Since his crime of felony murder was more serious than most of the other boys, he had a cell to himself. At least that made him feel a little safer. But how do you really feel safe in a place like this? Fred could have never imagined what it would be like. He never even thought of jail. He had just wanted to get away from his life on the chicken farm.

Right now, he would give anything to have that life back. He couldn't believe how one little mistake could have put him in this place. How was he to know that the store's owner would be inside with a gun, and would shoot at them?

He shivered and wrapped his lone blanket more tightly around himself. He wasn't sure if the shakes came because of the cold inside the jail, or because of the fear inside him. The cold cement floor and iron frame bed that hung from the concrete block walls seemed to seep a cold that he had never felt before. It chilled him to the bone. It enveloped him. He couldn't escape it.

When he saw Nelda and Hubert, it made this place seem worse. How could he have ever thought that his home was so bad? He had a warm bed, good hot meals, clean clothes and, most of all, some freedom.

He thought he would explode if he had to stay here much longer. He was ashamed in front of his parents. He missed his little sister, Jenny. He wanted to walk in the sunshine, kicking some rocks or lie on the damp grass. He even longed to walk through the chicken houses. The stench wouldn't seem so bad now.

Fred buried his face in his pillow to sob away the night, and cursed himself for thinking that life would be better somewhere else. He hadn't even thought of where he would sleep or how he would eat if he left home. "Idiot! Idiot!" he cried as he pummeled his pillow.

# Chapter 31

While Fred was crying in his pillow for the mess he had made out of his life, Donna was sitting on the floor in front of a roaring fire with a glass of wine and leaning against Paul. She was silently thanking God that he had given her such a wonderful, understanding and forgiving husband.

Paul had stood by her through all the ups and downs of her relationship with Jenny. He hurt with her and for her, but he wouldn't let himself be drawn into the self-deception that Jenny could ever be their child. He watched Donna pull herself out of her self-pity, when there was a need for action on behalf of the Moore family. Donna was good in a crisis. She was an excellent coordinator and had a very level head and analytical mind. She could pull all the right folks together to make something happen, and she did.

It was almost a miracle how she had motivated the church members to support the Moore family. Paul didn't quite understand it, but he knew that Donna's calm, patient understanding of people and her belief that people are innately good could be seen by the church leaders. He knew that her tenacity made them believe in her too. She had a way of inspiring people around her to do their best.

Their life at home was entirely theirs again. When she came in at night, Donna was ready to be his wife and to devote her evening to him and their life together. It was what he had prayed for all these months. Even their sex life was more spontaneous.

Paul had always loved his job and the hours he must spend to keep on top of the details of running a manufacturing plant. He loved Donna and their life. The only thing missing was a child, in his mind the symbol of a happy home. He rarely talked about this void to Donna because he knew how fragile she was on the subject. But tonight he wanted to open his heart to her and let her know how important it was to him that they begin planning for a family again. He would be fine if they had to adopt a child. He could love a child born to someone else. He and Donna would make that child part of their family.

Soft semi-classical music was playing in the background. They hadn't said much since dinner. They were enjoying their closeness and the peace and quiet of the evening.

"Donna."

"Huh," she said sleepily.

"The night is so peaceful and romantic. Would you want to disturb our life with a baby?"

She bolted upright away from him, a big smile on her face, "Oh, you know that's what I want more than anything. Are we ready to face potential disappointment again?"

"I am if you are. Our life is perfect, except for the sound of little feet running across the floor."

"It will be hard. We will be on edge the whole 9 months."

"I know. But the doctor told us that we had everything working in our favor for a normal pregnancy this time. I think we will regret it if we don't try again. And, if for some reason, we can't get pregnant or something happens, God forbid, to this baby, I'm open to looking at adoption."

"Me too. After falling in love with Jenny, I know that I can love a child as my own even if I didn't give birth to it. I'm so glad you're ready for this too. I was so afraid that you would never want to take a chance on us having that pain again."

She nestled against Paul again and they spent the rest of the evening lost in their own dreams of their life with a child.

# Chapter 32

Mr. Kittenridge had not been surprised at the speed at which the Grand Jury had indicted Fred. But he was surprised at how quickly the case was placed on the docket for trial. In his experience, he had never been able to get a speedy trial. In this case, he really didn't want a quick trial. He felt that the longer he could postpone it, the more the townspeople would forget the horror of the accident that had killed Bob.

And he truly felt that it had been an accident. Fred had not intended for Bob or the store's owner to get hurt. In his adolescent way, he was trying to get attention. Mr. Kittenridge didn't think that Fred really wanted to run away. He was just looking for some reassurance that he would be missed if he left. All kids felt that way at some point in their teenage years. But not all kids acted out the way Fred had.

Why? What made Fred carry out a plan that other teenagers would only brag about doing? How could it have been that bad at home or at school? It was still hard to understand teenagers' actions.

He also had many questions about Donna Whitsfield and how she had become such a big part of the family. Nelda didn't seem to have any great feelings for Donna. Hubert was ambivalent toward her. It was only Jenny that seemed to have some tie to her. Their relationship was deeper than teacher-student. And Donna wasn't her teacher. It just didn't seem right. But he was thankful for Donna's help. He would have had to pay someone to do all the typing Donna had done. And he didn't know where the money would have come from. With him working here, he was not bringing in any income from his practice in Atlanta. He went back to his home every other weekend to check on things and take care of his practice. He had virtually retired anyway, but there were a few collection cases he retained to help pay his bills.

When he realized he had been daydreaming, he shook his head to clear away the cobwebs. His concentration needed to be dedicated to Fred for now. The other stuff would sort itself out as time went along.

His defense was going to be "accessory to felony breaking and entering." That would put some blame on the dead boy, but there was no other way. Since Fred had not been carrying the gun, the case could be made that he didn't know anything about it and had only agreed to participate in shoplifting. He would not put Fred on the stand. That way he could protect any statements that might be pulled out of him by the District Attorney.

If he could prove his position, the charges would be changed to a misdemeanor and Fred could get off with only probation. It was a long shot. But there was no other way. The storeowner was distraught that he had shot the other teenager. The DA didn't want to press charges against him, but felt that someone had to pay for the boy's death.

The stacks of hundreds of pages had been filed and the court day was here.

Mr. Kittenridge bowed his head and prayed that God would allow him to do his best in this trial. He needed to be prepared to help his grandson and to close this horrible chapter of history for the town.

## Chapter 33

Zeb Taylor looked out the window at the gray overcast sky.

"Perfect day for a trial." He thought. "Probably rain before I could get any hoeing done, and it's much too cold to fish. Fishing hasn't been too good lately anyhow. Wonder if the fish know something important is brewing."

The trial had the whole town in a tizzy. There hadn't been anything this exciting since the shooting Mrs. Milligan remembered from 20 years before.

The Grand Jury had not taken long to bring in an indictment against Fred Moore. There had been evidence enough: fingerprints, the gun, an eyewitness who saw two boys hanging around the station. And, of course, Roger Martin, the storeowner. The DA swiftly charged Fred with felony murder.

The second-degree murder charge stemmed out of the classification for a person who "recklessly engages in conduct which creates a grave risk of death and thereby causes the death of another person."

Zeb had been on lots of juries in his time; been foreman a handful of times. This was one jury he didn't want to be chosen for. It was far too important. A man's life was just too important. No, he didn't want to be called for this job at all.

As Donna walked toward the courthouse, she noticed the crowd already gathered on the lawn. She wondered why so many people came to gloat over someone else's troubles.

She pictured the courthouse, as it must have looked almost 70 years ago just before the Great Tornado of '36. This historic disaster almost destroyed the town. Debris was strewn for miles and 203 people were killed. Even the courthouse bell had been found 15 miles outside the city. It was now housed on a memorial in the lobby to remind the citizens of their history. In those days the courtyard at the courthouse was made for spending time. Benches were placed under draping branches to shade visitors or were placed strategically so that observers could watch the townspeople go about their business. Some folks just sat and watched people going in and out of the courthouse, creating rumors of what business they had inside the great building. Sometimes they would just sit and listen to one of the street-corner preachers who hung out on the square.

Now everything was too efficient to accommodate this crowd. There were a few benches in strategic places, but they did not invite anyone to sit and visit. Instead it was designed to be a busy, important place. It was not a place for wasting time. The incongruity of the scene made her hasten inside.

The lobby of the courthouse was new and designed specifically to provide adequate room to honor the historic bell that had rested on the lawn after the '36 tornado. As Donna walked through the security check-point she looked over at the impressive bell in the center of the lobby. She prayed that the bell of justice would ring for Fred and that he would be found not guilty.

As she walked into the lawyer's lounge looking for Mr. Kittenridge, she still had to pinch herself to face the reality that he had actually asked for her help. She knew that her secretarial skills were greatly needed in preparing the voluminous petitions interrogatories, affidavits and motions for this trial.

The more she had worked on the case the more she became determined to help Mr. Kittenridge obtain an acquittal. But this was not going to be easy. The town was primed for an exciting conclusion to the trial, and the jury could not be impartial, no matter how isolated they tried to keep them.

The gossip flowed freely from one clan to the other. Everyone had a theory on the case and the truth really didn't matter.

Donna had just completed typing an order to be filed with the court, asking for the district attorney's office to release evidence, which they had obtained in their preliminary investigation that would be beneficial to the defendant, Fred. Mr. Kittenridge was delighted to get the order so soon and met her at the door. "Donna, I don't know what we would do without you. This is really important to get filed today."

"I would have brought it over sooner, but there is a problem with parking around the courthouse."

"I know. I feel the tension in the air and the trial hasn't even begun."

Donna looked around at the animated faces as she and Jenny's grandfather walked into the courtroom. The room compressed with anticipation. Donna looked for Jenny's mother and father. They were seated directly behind the defense attorney's table. Nelda's head was held high. Hubert's was hanging just a little. He held his hat in his hands and slowly turned it, watching his hands work the rhythm, twisting it from hand to hand.

## Chapter 34

Sixty people had been chosen as the jury pool. Twelve individuals would decide the fate of this man-child. Donna wondered how Mr. Kittenridge would decide who to eliminate and who to leave as potential jurors. She trusted his experience and dedication to the case. But she was still scared. Scared for the little boy who sat wide-eyed, glancing furtively around as the jury pool and gawkers invaded the room. How could she protect him? Then she realized that if she felt this helpless and afraid, the Moores must feel so much more helpless and afraid.

How could she help them? How could she protect Jenny? Her head was spinning with the uncertainty for them.

Over the next few days the jury selection went quickly. There were no significant issues to reject the jurors over. This conservative community was known for even-tempered decisions by juries. The community had always been a safe place to live. Some people didn't even lock their doors. Most folks wanted it to remain that way. Juries handed out fair verdicts to deter crime. The judges followed the same philosophy with sentencing.

Every afternoon when he left the courthouse Mr. Kittenridge would go over to the jail and talk with Fred. His plan was to build his case around teenage pranks. He did not plan to put Fred on the stand. But Fred had been isolated long enough that he had his own ideas of how the trial should be handled. He wanted to acknowledge his part in the robbery and take the consequences of his deeds. He needed to accept this responsibility. He felt it was part of his punishment and would enable him to move forward with his life.

Mr. Kittenridge insisted, "Fred, you don't want to be put on the stand. The DA will turn everything you say against you."

"Grandpa, I know what you're trying to do. But it's time I stood up and took my licks. I was part of the robbery. I was there. I saw Bob die. Grandpa, he died!"

Mr. Kittenridge looked at Fred with pride and fear. He didn't want his grandson to go to jail, but he was so proud that he had owned-up to his mistakes. He guessed he would have to change his approach to the defense.

The trial began with the DA putting Roger Martin on the stand. Roger felt so guilty about shooting Bob that he wanted to testify against Fred. He needed to transfer his feeling of guilt to someone else. Fred was the logical person. As he was giving his testimony, Roger broke down. "I didn't mean to shoot that boy. I don't even remember pulling the trigger. I was just so determined that nobody would rob my store again. But when I saw him carrying that gun, my fear took control. He wasn't pointing the gun at me. I should have waited."

This testimony was a big shock to Mr. Kittenridge. Roger Martin had not said the things that he expected. He didn't even mention Fred. He only talked about his own guilt. Maybe his statements would help Fred instead of convicting him. Mr. Kittenridge decided not to cross-examine him.

The next witness for the prosecution was Bob's father. The loss of a son can make a man say a lot of things, even things that aren't true. Mr. Kittenridge was concerned over Mr. Lunsford's testimony. Once again, he was surprised.

"I planned to come here today because I felt that my son had been influenced by Fred Moore to do things he wouldn't normally do. I lost my son. I'll never see him again. It was a useless act that should have never happened. But I didn't know my son as well as I thought I did. Yesterday I found $50 hidden in Bob's room. Now, I can't prove it, but I think it was half of the $100 that was taken from Mr. Brown's store. Bob denied being part of that prank. But I should have known better. If he could do that, then he could be part of this other robbery. There has been enough pain because of this act. I don't want it to continue. I don't want to blame Fred. They were just both kids. Bob was older than Fred. He probably influenced him. I want this to be over. I need to bury my pain just like I've buried my son."

When Fred took the stand, there were surprised comments from the courtroom. Fred's grandfather asked him to tell exactly what happened that night. Fred recounted the events truthfully and without excuses. Then he ended his testimony with a full apology.

"Now I know that it was very stupid to think that running away would solve any problem. I was the one who asked Bob to help me rob Mr. Martin's station. I thought I wanted to get away from my life here. Since I've been in jail these past months, I realize how fortunate I am to have a family that loves me, a safe, warm place to live and good, hot food three meals a day. I've felt sorry for myself for no reason. I've got to start being a part of my family and stand with my parents like they've stood with me. I'm ready to face whatever punishment I get for being part of a crime. I just want you all to know how sorry I am about everything. When I get out of jail, I promise to be a law-abiding citizen and to help other teens make good decisions."

Reverend McClure took the stand in Fred's defense. He told the history of the Moore family and the church and how there would be no church in this location if it had not been for Hubert Moore. He also revealed that the family had been taken advantage of by the church congregation without their realizing it.

Because of the circumstances and Fred's age, Judge O'Brien decided that he would sentence Fred to two years' probation. 'He can attend school and must have a job. He also must do community service." Rev. McClure offered Fred a job at the church, doing cleanup and lawn maintenance. Since the church is next door to the Moore's house the judge was happy with that solution.

# Chapter 35

The May sun glistens off the ripples on the surface of Lake Lanier, bouncing rays back into the trees where Paul is grilling hamburgers. Donna glances over at her husband and is filled with so much love that it makes cold shivers down her spine to think what could have happened. If Paul had been a different man, he wouldn't have stood by her during her infatuation with Jenny. He might have left her to find her own way. But Paul was not the kind of man who gives up on the people he loves. Just like God had not given up on her or Fred. Paul felt Donna's eyes on him and gave her his beautiful smile.

Fred had become a kind, gentle young man. He was abiding by the ruling of the judge and was completing his school classes despite some students' harassment. He found that he enjoyed working on the church grounds. He liked the feeling he got when he planted the small plants and watched them flourish as he fertilized and watered them. He might just become a landscaper. The church grounds were more defined now, since the church bought the property on the right side of the church for additional parking. That acreage had been sitting unattended for years. The widowed owner had been in a nursing home. When she recently died, her family wanted to sell it because they had all moved away from Gainesville and had no desire to maintain ownership. The church eagerly purchased the acreage and began work immediately on paving it for parking. However, the parking lot was laid out with generous consideration for the Moore family. There were buffer zones of spruce trees to hide the asphalt from the view at the Moore's house.

Now, Jenny and Fred were down at the water's edge fishing and laughing at the twigs and brush they caught, thinking each time that it was a big fish. They had become close and were very protective of each other and their relationship. They both knew that they had almost lost each other.

Nelda helped Donna put out the rest of the picnic food and set the table with plastic plates and glasses. Hubert was lying in the hammock under the sweeping oak tree near the back deck of the cabin. He said he was guarding the chilling watermelon in the ice chest to be sure no one got into it before lunch.

This was the kind of day Donna had looked forward to since she and Paul bought the cabin. They had not enjoyed the cabin with friends because until now they had no true friends in Gainesville. Nelda and Hubert and their family were becoming the center of Donna and Paul's social life in Gainesville, even though Donna and Paul were making new friends at the First Baptist Church. Donna felt at home in the large church and Paul was enjoying the sermons. He and Donna were back to analyzing the sermons over Sunday lunch each week.

It was a peaceful day. The slight breeze rustled the leaves on the trees, making the filtered sun highlight the early blooms of azaleas, African irises, dianthuses, pansies and lilies. Their colors seemed to burst forth each time the sun struck their hiding places in the yard. The mild temperature held back the mosquitoes and wasps. It was a perfect day for a picnic.

Nelda leaned close to Donna and whispered, "Are you still having that mornin' nausea?"

"It's not so bad now. The doctor says it will go away soon. But I'd endure anything for this baby. Sometimes I can't believe how God has blessed me. Not only do I have a second family here with you, Hubert, Fred and Jenny, but now I will have my own child. I hope that Paul and I can be good parents like you and Hubert are." Donna's face reddened slightly at the memory of her initial impressions of Nelda abusing Jenny.

"There's no doubt. You've been waiting a long time for this baby. I can't wait until my father gets here so you can tell him. You know that he thinks of you as a second daughter. And I think of you as a sister. I don't know what we would have done during Fred's ordeal and trial without your support and friendship. We'll never be able to repay you."

"You just wait until this baby is born. I'm calling on you to help baby sit until Jenny is old enough to leave the baby with her. You're not going to get off easy."

"There's nothing that would make me prouder than to help you with your baby."

They all turned at the sound of tires on the dirt driveway. Mr. Kittenridge had arrived to complete the family gathering. Donna was the first to walk up to the car to help him unload cake and ice cream and to tell him her news.

Life was good!

# Epilogue

As Donna applied her eye liner, she caught the reflection of Paul in the bathroom mirror, lifting Ramona out of her crib. The look on his face was pure love. Ramona smiled back at her dad and made happy cooing sounds.

The year had passed so quickly. Donna could never have imagined how a baby can change your life. Paul no longer went to the golf course every Sunday. In fact, he played golf very seldom now and when he did it was always on a Saturday or after work. He wanted to spend every minute away from work with his wife and daughter.

Paul began spending weekends with Donna long before Ramona was born. They reconnected like they had been when they first married. He told Donna that the reason he had spent all his Sundays playing golf was because he hurt so much about losing their baby and he couldn't stand to see Donna mourning after so long a time. He felt his family was whole now.

The pregnancy had not been difficult. The doctor even told them that there was no reason they couldn't have another baby. They agreed they would wait a while to try again. During her pregnancy Donna had discovered a not-for-profit group that was growing in the Gainesville-Hall/Dawson Counties supporting children that were having difficulties at home and representing and advocating for them in the court system. Trained volunteers would interview family members, schools, churches, neighbors and the child to gather information. As the Department of Family and Children Services received referrals about home issues involving children a volunteer would get involved and got to court and testify as the child's advocate based on the facts they obtained in the interviews. Donna learned everything she could about this group, Court Appointed Special Advocate (CASA) and decided to become one of these advocates. While pregnant she was trained and advocated for two separate children in court. She wished there had been a group like this available when she had first met Jenny. She could have helped the Moores in a more positive way with this background. She vowed that she would find a way to keep this volunteer work a part of her life for a long time. It was so helpful to the judge when making custody decisions about children and their families.

"Paul, honey, we need to get a move on. We'll be late for church. Nelda and Hubert will try to save us a seat, but so many new folks are coming to the church now, I'm not sure they will be able to hold our place."

"Okay, Mommy. I'll hurry. Just can't seem to put this little sweetheart down."

"I know. We are so blessed. I can hardly believe the year we've had. The church helped Hubert get a loan to update the chicken houses so they could get a new contract for broiler chickens. The profits he is making each time he grows the chicks into a suitable weight for the processing plant has allowed them to be financially independent. Fred has completed his probation and is continuing to work at the church maintaining the grounds and has been accepted by the technical school to study landscape construction. I'm so proud of him. That's why we must be on time, in order to see him get his Achievement Award at church."

"And I want to hear Jenny play the piano for the church. She has really blossomed this year with her lessons. I think she just might be a natural. I'm proud of her, too." Paul pulled his tie tight and grabbed Donna as she walked passed him.

"I'm so thankful God brought us to this city, this church and the Moore family. He knew what we needed to make our lives complete. I'm ashamed I doubted that He was always working for our good. We're home in every sense of the word." Donna kissed Paul and took her precious daughter from him as they made their way to the car.

# Book Review

One of the most rewarding things for an author is for their story to come alive under a new set of eyes.

Betty Smith (friend, teacher, mother, grandmother, supporter and Christian woman extraordinaire) did that with her suggestions for **Rescuing Jenny.** Her life experiences and world travels gave her a vision as to how the book could be used by teachers, parents and hurting adults to analyze child abuse and define what that phrase means to them. And then to decide what they should do about it, if they ever saw it.

This book offers an opportunity to think about child abuse and/or neglect and the appearance of child abuse. There are nuisances we all may see from time to time that make us think a child is being abused. How would you answer these questions?

# Questions

Thoughts to discuss:

1. What is abuse?
2. What should Donna have done to help Jenny?
3. What was Donna's motivation for rescuing Jenny?
4. What was the church's relationship with the Moore family?
5. How could the church have helped Jenny?
6. Who gets to determine what abuse is?
7. How was the whole Moore family abused by the church?
8. How should Christian values be applied in this situation?
9. Are we all guilty of neglect in some areas?
10. When should DFACS be called in a potential abuse case?

## ABOUT THE AUTHOR

As a full-time working Mom, Loraine Haynie had little time to devote to her writing passion. After retirement she achieved her dream of being a full-time author.

A dozen years earlier she visited a small church and saw a little disheveled girl with her Mom and was enchanted by the child. For years she thought about this little girl and what her life must be like. Donna Whitsfield was born in those moments and became a close friend to Loraine's imagination, along with the little girl, Jenny.

Rescuing Jenny is Loraine's second published book. Her first book, All the Way, is a memoir of her mother's life and was published in 2017.

Loraine holds a bachelor's degree in Journalism and worked in various positions, including 20 years in a local hospital, during her career. She is working on her third book which should be available late spring of 2018. Her fourth book is in research development.

She and her husband, Billy, stay busy living in an Active Adult Community in Hoschton, Georgia.

Made in the USA
Columbia, SC
12 January 2019